1980

Happy Christmas
   Enjoy the

love Mary · Gary

THE DOLMEN BOOK OF
IRISH CHRISTMAS STORIES

THE DOLMEN BOOK OF

Irish Christmas Stories

Edited by Dermot Bolger

Ann Devlin
Brian Lynch
Pat McCabe
John McGahern
Bernard McLaverty
Michael MacLaverty
Aisling Maguire
Frank O'Connor
Sean O'Faolain
James Plunkett
William Trevor
Anthony C. West

THE DOLMEN PRESS

*Set in Palatino type by Redsetter Limited
and produced by Keats European Production Limited
for the publisher*

The Dolmen Press Limited
Mountrath, Portlaoise, Ireland

Designed by Liam Miller

First published 1986

ISBN 0 85105 456 0

The Dolmen Press receives financial assistance from
The Arts Council, An Comhairle Ealaíon, Ireland

CONTENTS

ACKNOWLEDGEMENTS

The publisher and the editor wish to thank the following, for permission to include copyright material in this book.

Whimsical Beasts, Aisling Maguire. *Christmas Morning*, Frank O'Connor, A. D. Peters & Co. *No Fatted Calf*, Anthony C. West. *Two of a Kind*, Sean O'Faolain, A. P. Watt Ltd. *The Time of Year*, William Trevor, A. D. Peters & Co. *Father Christmas*, Michael McLaverty from *Collected Short Stories*, Poolbeg Press. *Apaches*, Pat McCabe. *The Journey to Somewhere Else*, Ann Devlin, from *The Way Paver*, Faber & Faber Ltd. *Finegan's Ark*, James Plunkett. *A Present for Christmas*, Bernard MacLaverty from *Secrets*, Blackstaff Press. *Curtains for Christmas*, Brian Lynch. *Christmas*, John McGahern from *Nightlines*, Faber & Faber Ltd.

WHIMSICAL BEASTS

AISLING MAGUIRE

He kept her on the outskirts of the city in a flat fifteen floors up from the ground. Here he had given rein to every whim of his fantasy, masking the blind concrete walls with swags of red crepe so that it was impossible at night to tell where the doors and windows stood. He was terrified of losing her. He had happened upon her and, indeed, could even believe that he had created her.

She was nervous, shrinking always just a little from his kiss. That charmed him, her fretful reluctance to be possessed opening at length to a languorous unfolding of herself. She regarded him with implacable eyes and never spoke until he had spoken. She would take his coat, shake out the rain and hang it behind the door, and, once he was seated, she would remove his shoes and socks to chafe his cold, tired feet between her hands and lay her cheeks first on one, then on the other.

Still, he could not believe that she was there for him, no matter what time of the evening or the day he called. At the start, in his anxiety, he kept irregular hours, returning in the middle of the morning or at lunchtime. Sometimes he would leave the flat, go downstairs, wait half an hour, and go back up, yet he found her always there, seated by the window, maybe, staring out across the gaseous yellow sky of the city, if not there, she might be lying on the black platform bed that rose on a single strut in the corner of the room like an outlandish fungus sprung from

9

nowhere in the dead of night, or like an aerial sensitive to the atmosphere of the room and the fluctuation of their moods. Satisfied that she had composed herself to wait for him alone, he would leave again, the fast beat of his heart slackening down to an empty pace.

What she did while she was there during the day was a matter of indifference to him. He sensed, however, that her mind was not one which required great stimulation. The few newspapers that he brought home she would remove from his coat pocket, spread on the floor and, sitting cross-legged, with her elbows on her knees, and her jowls pressed into the palms of her hands, she would gaze unmoving at the pages. For a few evenings he watched her do this and, occasionally, with one finger trace the contour of the faces in the photographs, until it occurred to him that, perhaps, she could not read. She looked at him, half-smiling when he asked her and shook her head.

The letters on those pages, he thought, must appear as alien to her as the characters of Cyrillic or Arabic script to me. He was pleased that she could not read for it set a further obstacle in the path of her potential escape.

'What does it look like to you, all that writing?' he asked.

For a moment she deliberated, pulling at a twist of hair that fell to the nape of her neck, then grinned. 'Like millions of tiny insects marching up and down in rows,' she replied, and imitated the walk of a spider with her fingers on the page.

It was when he took up smoking again that he discovered her one peculiar habit or talent, he was not sure which it should be called, for her fingers worked with such alacrity that their movement seemed completely unwilled like the reflexive spasms of palsy. An accumulation of small gold animals proceeded from this incessant fidgetting· As soon as a packet of cigarettes had been discarded she would pounce and, with her finger and thumb slide the gold foil from the box. He thought at first that she was going to make a mock goblet plugged at the base with moistened whitepaper so that by a quick upswing of the wrist it could adhere to the ceiling, like those that stud the stained plaster of countless pubs. Had she done that he would have been disgusted and enraged, the sight of an object so useless and vulgar, repulsive to his taste. Contrary to this, he was enchanted by her creative knack, as she presented him with a golden peacock in full display.

Each evening a new specimen was added to the collection until she was pushed at last to invent new sub-species, with the features of various animals assembled in comical or grotesque shapes that recalled ancient hieroglyphs. As the dark nights of winter descended he found himself to be more and more beguiled by the glow that shone, in the reflected light of the gas stove, from this fanciful troop. She could spend hours stretched on the floor shifting the tiny creatures in an intricate choreography and her narrow greenish eyes as she stared into the pattern of movements gave back greenish flecks of golden light. Only when he might stroke her hair or touch her cheeks would she advert again to his presence and then she would reach up, take his hand, open it, and place one creature from her fragile menagerie on his palm. He accepted them as tokens of her feeling for him and when night had finally come and the lights were turned out he felt her in his arms become a miraculous exotic beast.

That she should have an artistic flair gratified him,

for it seemed to redound on his credit that he should have isolated her out of the drift of vagabonds that ranged the streets. He was even moved to think that he would like to take her out, and parade her on his arm down the avenues as a man of property might do, but was brought up short by the fear that she might then expect this promenade to become a regular part of their affair. He was unwilling to disrupt the singular calm they had achieved in their fifteenth floor rooms. Besides, there was the problem of clothes, he would have to dress her in the costume of the rich and, for himself, would have to find a tailor-made suit with knife edge creases, and replace his inelegant grey coat with one of camel-hair or vicuna.

No, it was better to remain aloft, balanced above the city in their crow's nest, and improvise the forests and boulevards of the world in the interlocked shafts and hollows of their limbs. Instead of taking her out he brought her a gift. The parcel contained four miniature oriental screens he had spied one morning in the corner of an antique shop window. Each one was made of a piece of outstretched silk held in a black wooden frame standing on scroll-shaped feet. The brilliance of their primary colours attracted him, the red, the blue, the yellow and the green, as bright as jewels that flashed under the passage of light. She laughed when she saw them, and placed them in a line on the window-sill just to watch the tints leap and change like the shudder of colour on a bird's feathers.

Soon the screens were incorporated into the manoeuvres of the golden menagerie, and composed as backdrop of flats as in theatrical scenery. The movements of the animals now took on a narrative form as their comings and goings in front of and around the screens followed the routines of coincidence and conflict intrinsic to the oldest plots of all.

He wondered how far her range would extend and, in consequence, smoked more than he craved and certainly more than was healthy but there was no limit to the procession of creatures that issued from her hands. Birds and beasts of inimaginable aspect, crowned with horns, or flowering with layered wings, her multiple variations on the order of nature baffled him. Unmindful of it himself, he was becoming physically derelict in the service of her art. He was aware of bouts of coughing that shook his lungs till warm phlegm curdled at the back of his mouth. His pallor, he knew, had waned from a moderate ruddiness to a feeble grey. This much the people at the garment factory where he worked had told him, remarking with meaningless concern on the decline in his complexion, but he was dismissive, attributing any alteration in his person to the onset of winter. The deposit of nicotine in his lungs consumed his energy and the new slowness of his movements interposed a veil of hesitancy between himself and his mistress.

Then, one evening, she surprised him with a request for a child. He halted in the act of drawing the red curtain and kept his eyes bent to the city which, in the amorphous gathering of dusk was condensed to the shape of a massive engine, ignited here and there by the sodium glow of the street lamps.

'So, this is what it comes to,' he thought and recognised that the plethora of whimsical animal figures had been an elaborate prelude to this ingenuous suggestion. She wa little more than a child herself. He was aware too, in passing, of the season, and the notion took hold of him that somehow the mood of the city, in its swagger of Christmas fare, had percolated through the unpleasant welter of drizzle, smoke and noise, to this high enclosure and had impressed itself on her senses, stirring there the itch for a child. He

13

closed the curtain and turned to face her.

'Why do you want a child?' he asked.

She shrugged and bent her head.

'For company,' her eyes swung across to the display of golden animals on the floor.

'Yes, that's all you need now in your collection, isn't it?'

She nodded.

'But it's more than that too,' she protested and splayed her hand over her flat stomach.

'Well, I don't,' he said. 'A child would only bring confusion in here.'

He mounted the ladder onto the platform bed and lay with his face to the corner but did not sleep. On the floor below him she sat, moving her cast of animals about in the pale gleam of the gas flame, and watched as broad shadows were flung against the wall and ceiling.

In the twelve day approach to Christmas carol singers clutered on the thoroughfares and the savour of mince pies sold at outdoor stalls enriched the customary dank smell of the city. Occasionally, some of these festive singers and traders turned up in the grey outer housing zones. For those in the vulgar flats the voices of the carol singers lost all coherence, the notes and words of their songs distorted by the scarfing currents of air trapped between the tall concrete blocks.

He observed a growing vagueness in her eyes and began on another evening to defend himself. 'I had children once,' he said. 'As you might have guessed, from a marriage of twenty years. They have their moments I grant you, a trick of the voice or a look that can win your heart. But they can torment your nerves too, and when they find the weak spot they persist until you no longer know what it is you are saying or doing. You are all the children I need now.'

'But me,' was all that she said, and rubbed a clear space in the condensation on the glass as she tried to recompose in her head the dissonant notes that rose at intervals from the huddle of young carol singers in the darkness below.

'It would have been nice to have thrown some money to them,' she remarked when the singers had moved away.

'Yes, and falling from this height the coins would probably have killed them.'

She withdrew from the window and let the curtain resettle, flush with its pair.

He rarely moved now from the bed. Once in the door he undressed and climbed onto the platform. The illness that had swamped his lungs was becoming chronic. When he breathed he felt a wound stretch inside and supurate, striking up a rattle in his chest. His skin had dried and drawn in to meet his bones. From where he lay he instructed her with monarchical detachment in the preparation of their supper but her disinterest angered him and he redoubled the rate of his smoking. As each carton was emptied he would toss it down to her, and, straightaway, her fingers would begin to manipulate the slim gold paper. His eyes then would be held by her deft movements and his attitude would once more soften towards her.

Despite his illness, he continued to work, shrugging his weakened frame into the grey coat. It did not snow in the city but a hard frost bound the roofs and roads and pavements like sheets of iron. Even in those last days before Christmas he forced himself out and back at the same hour, morning and evening, resolved not to admit of any change, for reasons of health or merrymaking, in the daily course he had established. Only by conducting each day in the same way could he uphold the pretence that time did not pass.

It was on Christmas Eve that she left him. What few material trappings she possessed were tied into a length of the red curtain and the bizarre hoards of gold foil animals was neatly pocketed in gaps and folds of the cloth. The screens alone were left behind, placed in a square like a lidless box on the centre of the eating table, where a low bolt of sunlight struck through the exposed window making their colours appear almost transparent.

When she stepped onto the pavement she shivered as much from fear as from the first sting of the winter air. She moved towards the city, skirting the main routes in case, by hazard, he would choose to surprise her and return early on this one day. Being without money she was forced to walk and the drag of the red bundle on her shoulders retarded her pace so that dusk had fallen by the time she had reached the heart of the city. In a square that she recognised she halted to sit on a step and rub her feet, swollen now with the unaccustomed exercise, and bruised with the cold. From the top of the bundle, which she had placed on the ground beside her, gleamed a fragment of gold. She smiled, and, standing again, caught the glance of a child's face through an upper floor window. As she bent to pick up her bundle she extracted the delicate beast and placed it where she had been sitting.

Frost continued to fall that night in greater profusion than it had before, and a greenish vapour pervaded every quarter of the city, merging with the scant light that showed through shutters and hallways. No traffic broke the quiet but, lining the streets, on doorsteps and on windowsills, stood a myriad of minute golden creatures, each one astir with the playful flicker of new life.

CHRISTMAS MORNING

FRANK O'CONNOR

I never really liked my brother, Sonny. From the time he was a baby he was always the mother's pet and always chasing her to tell her what mischief I was up to. Mind you, I was usually up to something. Until I was nine or ten I was never much good at school, and I really believe it was to spite me that he was so smart at his books. He seemed to know by instinct that this was what Mother had set her heart on, and you might almost say he spelt himself into her favour.

'Mummy,' he'd say, 'will I call Larry in to his t-e-a?' or: 'Mummy, the k-e-t-e-l is boiling,' and, of course, when he was wrong she'd correct him, and next time he'd have it right and there would be no standing him. 'Mummy,' he'd say, 'aren't I a good speller?' Cripes, we could all be good spellers if we went on like that!

Mind you, it wasn't that I was stupid. Far from it. I was just restless and not able to fix my mind for long on any one thing. I'd do the lessons for the year before, or the lessons for the year after: what I couldn't stand were the lessons we were supposed to be doing at the time. In the evenings I used to go out and play with the Doherty gang. Not, again, that I was rough, but I liked the excitement, and for the life of me I couldn't see what attracted Mother about education.

'Can't you do your lessons first and play after?' she'd say, getting white with indignation. 'You ought to be ashamed of yourself that your baby brother can

17

read better than you.'

She didn't seem to understand that I wasn't, because there didn't seem to me to be anything particularly praiseworthy about reading, and it struck me as an occupation better suited to a sissy kid like Sonny.

'The dear knows what will become of you,' she'd say. 'If only you'd stick to your books you might be something good like a clerk or an engineer.'

'I'll be a clerk, Mummy,' Sonny would say smugly.

'Who wants to be an old clerk?' I'd say, just to annoy him. 'I'm going to be a soldier.'

'The dear knows, I'm afraid that's all you'll ever be fit for,' she would add with a sigh.

I couldn't help feeling at times that she wasn't all there. As if there was anything better a fellow could be!

Coming on to Christmas, with the days getting shorter and the shopping crowds bigger, I began to think of all the things I might get from Santa Claus. The Dohertys said there was no Santa Claus, only what your father and mother gave you, but the Dohertys were a rough class of children you wouldn't expect Santa to come to anyway. I was rooting round for whatever information I could pick up about him, but there didn't seem to be much. I was no hand with a pen, but if a letter would do any good I was ready to chance writing to him. I had plenty of initiative and was always writing off for free samples and prospectuses.

'Ah I don't know will he come at all this year,' Mother said with a worried air. 'He has enough to do looking after steady boys who mind their lessons without bothering about the rest.'

'He only comes to good spellers, Mummy,' said Sonny. 'Isn't that right?'

'He comes to any little boy who does his best, whether he's a good speller or not,' Mother said firmly.

Well, I did my best. God knows I did! It wasn't my fault if, four days before the holidays, Flogger Dawley gave us sums we couldn't do, and Peter Doherty and myself had to go on the lang. It wasn't for the love of it, for, take it from me, December is no month for mitching, and we spent most of our time sheltering from the rain in a store on the quays. The only mistake we made was imagining we could keep it up till the holidays without being spotted. That showed real lack of foresight.

Of course, Flogger Dawley noticed and sent home word to know what was keeping me. When I came in on the third day the mother gave me a look I'll never forget, and said: 'Your dinner is there.' She was too full to talk. When I tried to explain to her about Flogger Dawley and the sums she brushed it aside and said: 'You have no word.' I saw then it wasn't the langing she minded but the lies, though I still didn't see how you could lang without lying. She didn't speak to me for days. And even then I couldn't make out what she saw in education, or why she wouldn't let me grow up naturally like anyone else.

To make things worse, it stuffed Sonny up more than ever. He had the air of one saying: 'I don't know what they'd do without me in this blooming house.' He stood at the front door, leaning against the jamb with his hands in his trouser pockets, trying to make himself look like Father, and shouted to the other kids so that he could be heard all over the road.

'Larry isn't left go out. He went on the lang with Peter Doherty and me mother isn't talking to him.'

And at night, when we were in bed, he kept it up.

'Santa Claus won't bring you anything this year,

19

aha!'

'Of course he will,' I said.

'How do you know?'

'Why wouldn't he?'

'Because you went on the lang with Doherty. I wouldn't play with them Doherty fellows.'

'You wouldn't be left.'

'I wouldn't play with them. They're no class. They had the bobbies up to the house.'

'And how would Santa know I was on the lang with Peter Doherty?' I growled, losing patience with the little prig.

'Of course he'd know. Mummy would tell him.'

'And how could Mummy tell him and he up at the North Pole? Poor Ireland, she's rearing them yet! 'Tis easy seen you're only an old baby.'

'I'm not a baby, and I can spell better than you, and Santa won't bring you anything.'

'We'll see whether he will or not,' I said sarcastically, doing the old man on him.

But, to tell the God's truth, the old man was only bluff. You could never tell what powers these superhuman chaps would have of knowing what you were up to. And I had a bad conscience about the langing because I'd never seen the mother like that.

That was the night I decided that the only sensible thing to do was to see Santa myself and explain to him. Being a man, he'd probably understand. In those days I was a good-looking kid and had a way with me when I liked. I had only to smile nicely at the old gent on the North Mall to get a penny from him, and I felt if only I could get Santa by himself I could do the same with him and maybe get something worthwhile from him. I wanted a model railway: I was sick of Ludo and Snakes-and-Ladders.

I started to practise lying awake, counting five

hundred and then a thousand, and trying to hear first eleven, then midnight from Shandon. I felt sure Santa would be round by midnight seeing that he'd be coming from the north, and would have the whole of the south side to do afterwards. In some ways I was very farsighted. The only trouble was the things I was farsighted about.

I was so wrapped up in my own calculations that I had little attention to spare for Mother's difficulties. Sonny and I used to go to town with her, and while she was shopping we stood outside a toyshop in the North Main Street, arguing about what we'd like for Christmas.

On Christmas Eve when Father came home from work and gave her the housekeeping money, she stood looking at it doubtfully while her face grew white.

'Well?' he snapped, getting angry. 'What's wrong with that?'

'What's wrong with it?' she muttered. 'On Christmas Eve!'

'Well,' he asked truculently, sticking his hands in his trouser pockets as though to guard what was left, 'do you think I get more because it's Christmas?'

'Lord God,' she muttered distractedly. 'And not a bit of cake in the house, nor a candle, nor anything!'

'All right,' he shouted, beginning to stamp. 'How much will the candle be?'

'Ah, for pity's sake,' she cried, 'will you give me the money and not argue like that before the children? Do you think I'll leave them with nothing on the one day of the year?'

'Bad luck to you and your children!' he snarled. 'Am I to be slaving from one year's end to another for you to be throwing it away on toys? Here,' he added, tossing two half-crowns on the table, 'that's all you're going to get, so make the most of it.'

'I suppose the publicans will get the rest,' she said bitterly.

Later she went into town, but did not bring us with her, and returned with a lot of parcels, including the Christmas candle. We waited for Father to come home to his tea, but he didn't, so we had our own tea and a slice of Christmas cake each, and then Mother put Sonny on a chair with the holy-water stoup to sprinkle the candle, and when he lit it she said: 'The light of heaven to our souls.' I could see she was upset because Father wasn't in – it should be the oldest and the youngest. When we hung up our stockings at bedtime he was still out.

Then began the hardest couple of hours I ever put in. I was mad with sleep but afraid of losing the model railway, so I lay for a while, making up things to say to Santa when he came. They varied in tone from frivolous to grave, for some old gents like kids to be modest and well spoken, while others prefer them with spirit. When I had rehearsed them all I tried to wake Sonny to keep me company, but that kid slept like the dead.

Eleven struck from Shandon, and soon after I heard the latch, but it was only Father coming home.

'Hello, little girl,' he said, letting on to be surprised at finding Mother waiting for him, and then broke into a self-conscious giggle. 'What has you up so late?'

'Do you want your supper?' she asked shortly.

'Ah, no, no,' he replied. 'I had a bit of a pig's cheek at Daneen's on my way up.' (Daneen was my uncle.) 'I'm very fond of a bit of pig's cheek . . . My goodness, is it that late?' he exclaimed, letting on to be astonished. 'If I knew that I'd have gone to the North Chapel for midnight Mass. I'd like to hear the *Adeste* again. That's a hymn I'm very fond of – a most touching hymn.'

22

Then he began to hum in falsetto.

Adeste fideles
Solus domus dagus.

Father was very fond of Latin hymns, particularly
when he had a drop in him, but as he had no notion of
the words he made them up as he went along, and this
always drove Mother mad.

'Ah, you disgust me!' she said in a scalded voice,
and closed the room door behind her. Father laughed
as if he thought it a great joke; and he struck a match
to light his pipe and for a while puffed at it noisily.
The light under the door dimmed and went out but he
continued to sing emotionally.

Dixie medearo
Tutum tonum tantum
Venite adoremus.

He had it all wrong but the effect was the same on
me. To save my life I couldn't keep awake.

Coming on to dawn, I woke with the feeling that
something dreadful had happened. The whole house
was quiet, and the little bedroom that looked out on
the foot and a half of back yard was pitch-dark. It was
only when I glanced at the window that I saw how all
the silver had drained out of the sky. I jumped out of
bed to feel my stocking, well knowing that the worst
had happened. Santa had come while I was asleep,
and gone away with an entirely false impression of
me, because all he had left me was some sort of book,
folded up, a pen and pencil, and a tuppeny bag of
sweets. Not even Snakes-and-Ladders! For a while I
was too stunned even to think. A fellow who was able
to drive over rooftops and climb down chimneys

without getting stuck – God, wouldn't you think he'd know better?

Then I began to wonder what that foxy boy, Sonny, had. I went to his side of the bed and felt his stocking. For all his spelling and sucking-up he hadn't done so much better, because, apart from a bag of sweets like mine, all Santa had left him was a popgun, one that fired a cork on a piece of string and which you couild get in any huxter's shop for sixpence.

All the same, the fact remained that it was a gun, and a gun was better than a book any day of the week. The Dohertys had a gang, and the gang fought the Strawberry Lane kids who tried to play football on our road. That gun would be very useful to me in many ways, while it would be lost on Sonny who wouldn't be let play with the gang, even if he wanted to.

Then I got the inspiration, as it seemed to me, direct from heaven. Suppose I took the gun and gave Sonny the book! Sonny would never be any good in the gang: he was fond of spelling, and a studious child like him could learn a lot of spellings from a book like mine. As he hadn't seen Santa ny more than I had, what he hadn't seen wouldn't grieve him. I was doing no harm to anyone; in fact, if Sonny only knew, I was doing him a good turn which he might have cause to thank me for later. That was one thing I was always keen on; doing good turns. Perhaps this was Santa's intention the whole time and he had merely become confused between us. It was a mistake that might happen to anyone. So I put the book, the pencil, and the pen into Sonny's stocking and the popgun into my own, and returned to bed and slept again. As I say, in those days I had plenty of initiative.

It was Sonny who woke me, shaking me to tell me that Santa had come and left me a gun. I let on to be surprised and rather disappointed in the gun, and to divert his mind from it made him show me his picture book, and cracked it up to the skies.

As I knew, that kid was prepared to believe anything, and nothing would do him then but to take the presents in to show Father and Mother. This was a bad moment for me. After the way she had behaved about the langing, I distrusted Mother, though I had the consolation of believing that the only person who could contradict me was now somewhere up by the North Pole. That gave me a certain confidence, so Sonny and I burst in with our presents, shouting: 'Look what Santa Claus brought!'

Father and Mother woke, and Mother smiled, but only for an instant. As she looked at me her face changed. I knew that look; I knew it only too well. It was the same look she had worn the day I came home from langing, when she said I had no word.

'Larry,' she said in a low voice, 'where did you get that gun?'

'Santa left it in my stocking, Mummy,' I said, trying to put on an injured air, though it baffled me how she guessed that he hadn't. 'He did, honest.'

'You stole it from that poor child's stocking while he was asleep,' she said, her voice quivering with indignation. 'Larry, Larry, how could you be so mean?'

'Now, now, now,' Father said deprecatingly, ''tis Christmas morning.'

'Ah,' she said with real passion, 'it's easy it comes to you. Do you think I want my son to grow up a liar and a thief?'

'Ah, what thief, woman?' he said testily. 'Have sense, can't you?' He was as cross if you interrupted him in his benevolent moods as if they were of the other sort, and this one was probably exacerbated by a feeling of guilt for his behaviour of the night before. 'Here, Larry,' he said, reaching out for the money on the bedside table, 'here's sixpence for you and one for Sonny. Mind you don't lose it now!'

But I looked at Mother and saw what was in her eyes. I burst out crying, threw the popgun on the floor, and ran bawling out of the house before anyone on the road was awake. I rushed up the lane beside the house and threw myself on the wet grass.

I understood it all, and it was almost more than I could bear; that there was no Santa Claus, as the Dohertys said, only Mother trying to scrape together a few coppers from the housekeeping; that Father was mean and common and a drunkard, and that she had been relying on me to raise her out of the misery of the life she was leading. And I knew that the look in her eyes was the fear that, like my father, I should turn out to be mean and common and a drunkard.

NO FATTED CALF

ANTHONY C. WEST

Bwrwrwrwrwrr . . .' Adam Finney said.

He kept making this sound with a burl of his numb lips. It helped him stay within himself, for his life wanted to wander away from his body into the trackless night.

Except that now and again it pulled on the bit of rope in his left hand, he hardly knew the little black bitch was beside him. It was an unseen living thing, a vital movement in the darkness on the end of the lead like his own life in the darkness of his body. Sometimes he forgot about the dog and was startled when lightly it brushed his leg. The night was bond black. He could not even mark the trees against the drizzling wet fleece of the sky and only knew he was on the road by its hardness under his numb feet. Many times he wandered on to the verge, stopping and feeling for the road again with a blind man's foot.

Frequently the dog crossed the rope over his shins, and he chucked the beast back with an impatient curse. He did not want her, and had he thought about it, he might well have loosed her. Sometimes a straggling brier clawed his legs, but he chucked at the dog all the same, blaming the innocent animal for his general predicament.

'Bwrwrwrr . . .' he breathed. 'Come back, damn ye!'

The bitch made a small whimpering yelp and hung back on the rope. He stopped and warned it seriously: 'Now, don't ye start makin' more trouble for me!' Then he hauled it forward.

27

Tucking the lapels of his light raincoat together under his chin, he shrugged his shoulders and went on, assessing warily the antics of the raw liquor that yawed through his body. As usual, while the drink only disturbed his sense of balance, it increased the activity of his mind. In fact, such times he would seem to have two heads: one to moil over past misdeeds and failures, while the other was left conveniently free to blow and boast.

Coldly totalling the immediate failures, head number one said, 'Well? What's to be done now? You walked into Bob Dowden's dwelling with the greatest of expectations. Was he not the cousin of your dear dead father? Was he not an old rich bachelor with a tidy farm? Instead of politely refusing that half pint of potheen, you had to down it on an empty belly to show what a man you were, and then you sat in with the boys at their twopenny spoil-five.'

'Bwrwrwrwrrr! God damn ye, will ye come here!'

'Talk about all the money you made and your glorious past and the women you had! What did you do? You shamed Dowden out of offering you bed and board this Christmas night, you did. Spoil-five is right! Never could resist a card, could you, or a drink, or a broad? The three of them have followed you with ruin your whole life through.'

'Adam Finney has a sense of humour,' said head number two.

'Aye! And what'll he do now – kid himself he's in an hotel or a feather bed? Agh! – sitting down and twisting a few poor farmers' boys out of their few bob, drinking a half gallon of mountain dew to win a half-bred shepherd bitch that he doesn't want. Wonderful!'

'The bitch is worth two pounds any time!' the second head defended.

'Bwrwrrrr!'

'Face up to it, Finney. You're a forgotten exile now, a lost man and a sinner. Time has stolen away your youth. Time is black and heavy upon you. Where are you going to lay your head this night?'

'Agh, whisht now! Ye can go to the sister's place? She'll be glad to see ye, man! Blood's thicker'n water. She'll welcome ye with open arms — her long-lost black sheep brother home from the world's wilderness. Ye'll be kinda hero!'

'Maryann?' he muttered.

'Like hell you will! She hates your guts. She'll never forgive you.'

'Agh! – time heals old sores!' He shrugged.

'In your present state and general decomposition? . . . Adam Finney have you no pride at all? Fifteen long and silent years? Fifteen *dozen* years wouldn't wipe clean your shame with her!'

'Arragh, she's happy now? Dowden says she has a new baby – the third it is. Not bad goin' for an old man well past seventy – three alive an' three dead. Old man's darlin': that's what she is. But what's wrong to stay with her over Christmas? Christmas is always Christmas an' Maryann won't want to mind anything about it now. Stay the night away an' leave with decency on the morrow an' give the childer the wee bitch for a present from their Uncle Adam.'

'Bwrwrwrrr . . .'

'Aye, Christmas Eve!' number one head said sadly. 'What did you come back at all for?'

'I came home, well, because I just damn well *wanted* to come home! Have I not a right to visit the place of me birth?'

'You haven't any rights left, Finney, me boy. You've devoured your rights.'

'I'm a proud an' a free man yet!'

'You're a bag of bad wind with a terrible sickness on it! You're a blown horse, Finney. You're at your tether's end.'

His body shivered, and he broke into a loose cough.

Then he heard the tinkle of running water, and stopped. He wanted a drink. His throat was dry after the potheen. He gazed myopically about and stumbled toward the water sounds, vaguely identifying the place as Templemore, an old monastery destroyed by Cromwell. This would be the overflow from Templemore. Well, a famous parish spring that had never admitted a drought.

He groped through the bushes for the beaten footpath, guided by the chirping water as it chuckled over the stones. He remembered the spring, a twelve-by-six-foot cave cut cleanly into the rock under a powerful curve of ashlar. 'Come on!' he grunted to the dog, dragging it stiff-legged after him.

He had a healthy respect for the well's depth. He could not see a thing under the trees. Dropping to his knees, he felt forward to the water's edge and wet his sleeve. Taking off his hat he scooped it full and drank deeply, the water tasting slightly of the sweetness of hair oil.

Satisfied, he sat back on his heels, belching, shaking the hat dry and putting it back on his head, the wet leather band a burning rim of coldness on his brow. The water made him queasy, stirring up the potheen's power again, and small sleety snow began to fall through the drizzle, touching his numb face. He struck a match to see the time, saw the snow falling, and muttered in the double after-darkness, 'Snowin' now, bigod . . . five to midnight.'

The bitch was whining; he could feel her trembling through the rope. 'Shut up!' he growled, and waited for a new dizziness to subside. He lit a cigarette but the first draw made him cough so much he threw the fag away, the smoke blending with the phlegm in his throat and tasting like tar.

He shuddered and got to his feet. There was an old tale about this spring. Two monks were sometimes seen coming to it in the dead of night, dragging a woman between them, holding her by the arms and pushing her head and shoulders under the water. Some of the old people believed the earth remembered deeds and murders; and Templemore's reputation was doubly unsavoury for the well's being on Will Curry's land. Will was an unsociable man.

A shrieking gust caught and would have spilled him, but he dropped to his hands and knees.

Twenty years ago Will had caught Adam progging the orchard with sister Maryann. Only sixteen, she was hipped and breasted like a woman. With her red hair blowing and her milk-white skin, she had a pile of rosy apples gathered in her skirt. She couldn't run with them, and Will caught her, carrying her back under his arm to beneath the tree Adam was in. With her kicking and screaming, he laughed and put her over his knee and pulled down her drawers, skelping her bare arse. *Never forgot the sight!*

'Or,' Finney cried into the wind, 'when I slid down the tree an' he grabbed me! I kicked the old goat in the groin, an' he got thick and choked me, an' I watched everything goin' black with a roarin' in me ears, but I couldn't tell him to stop.

'When I came to, he was plashin' water over me face here at the spring an' cryin', "God, I mighta kilt ye! God, I mighta kilt ye! What hell did ye kick me for?"'

'But he give us all the apples we could carry an' five bob to boot!'

Later that night he had staggered home, one side of the road the same as the other, Maryann was standing

31

at the fire warming herself in her night-gown.

Only this evening Dowden had said something about Will going sour and wild, taking tramps in off the road to manage for him, setting his house on fire in the horrors of drink, God rest his soul. A terrible rough man he was, Dowden said, able for twenty pints in an evening. But then he had found a hill of gold in Australia.

With a groan, Finney got to his feet and began picking his way back to the road but lying on the grass verges and lifting darkness a little. Now and again he reeled, pulling the dog after him. He tried to breathe shallowly, since a deep breath stabbed his chest like a knife and made him cough. He wanted to cough but kept it back for fear. He had coughed up blood once on the boat.

He was crying in his mind now, saying over and over, 'Some place to go, some place to go, a place to sleep, a room with a roof, a dry place to lie down, and sleep!'

Trying to keep away from him, the nervous dog looped the rope round his ankles. He blundered, hamstrung, across the road, trying to save himself from falling, hauling at the rope and drawing the terrified animal close to his legs. She unwound the rope again, leaping away the length of it and hawking him headfirst across a low wall . . . .

In the near distance he began to hear a loud voice roaring at cattle. It was old Will Curry's voice, and Finney bestirred himself. Will was waving a hurricane lamp and swearing at half a dozen bullocks as he tried to get them into a shed out of the weather. His excited dog pressed the beasts too hard, and they ran past the door, surging up the muddy lane towards Finney.

Finney stood nervously in the lane's mouth and

watched the blowing, shadowy beasts shuffle toward him in the darkness. He yelled and waved his arms and turned them, while Will lifted his lamp over his head, trying to see beyond its dim saucer of light. Reluctantly, Finney shouted for Will to stand below the shed and he would drive them back. The last person he wanted to meet on such a night was old Will Curry.

The lamp ceased its wild gyrations and cast the stilted shadows of Will's legs across the yard's pocked mud, and with Finney behind them the animals huffed suspiciously into the dark shed, the dog flitting back and forth at their heels.

Will slammed the door and turned a large stone on edge against it. He came over, holding up the lamp to Finney's face.

'Arragh, it's ye, Adam!' he roared, and Finney shrank back afraid. 'How are ye, man?'

The old man's beery breath was heavy on the air, and his drunken reeling bulk came close to tower over him.

'I'm well, Will,' he muttered. 'It has turned a bad night.' He was thinking he should have allowed the bullocks to find their own way back.

Will was agreeing. 'Aye – bad. I'm on'y back from the town meself.' Will belched and swayed and Finney watched the snow slant softly past the lamp.

'I'd better be getti' along, Will, before the snow's too thick underfoot.'

'Aye,' Will agreed absently. Then he looked up and shouted, 'Come in for a bit, man?' He reached out and caught Finney's arm with a great square hand that was hard and heavy as an iron ingot. 'Come in an' tell us your travels, man!' he cried, and his great fingers bit into Finney's flesh.

They walked slowly round the end of the dwelling

33

house, Will indifferent to the six-inch soupy cattle-mud sucking at their feet. He was still holding Finney's arm, not steering him so much as leaning on him; demanding to know how many high yallers Finney had coupled. Then he stopped short suddenly to ask in a loud and porter-spittled whisper did Finney know the ruse the aborigine women had used against the miners? 'They filt it with sand, bigod!' he answered with a shocked hiss.

Finney had the clear image of a female shaped like a sandglass, and Will mulled on shaking his head and repeating 'Sand bigod!' as he led the way round to the front door.

The kitchen was surprisingly tidy, the hearth swept clean with a big bright fire of logs upon it. The scum from a hugh three-legged cauldron of potatoes spilled over into the flames, the lid rising and falling with lugubrious sighs. The last time Finney had seen the room it was lit by a solitary candle in a bottle on the table – a filthy bachelor shambles with cast-off clothes draped on every chair and a heap of strong socks by the darkened fireside. Now the whitewashed walls seemed lofty, illuminated as they were by the clean double-burner paraffin reflector that hung from a peg on one of them.

Will had aged, his giant's shoulders rounding a little, and his great barrel of a body was much thinner. His face was even lean, and in the fire's flicker it seemed pared down to the bone.

Will's black collie dog had crept through the open door and slunk over near the fire, making itself small in a dim corner and licking its wet paws. Finney did not want to stay and yet was glad of the shelter. While dreading the long laborious trek up snow-covered Templemore Hill and down again, and then across windswept Tullaghmore Bog where green will-o'-the-wisps gambolled and the road quaked underfoot, he wanted to go home. He was about to say that he wanted to go home when Will roared, 'Peg?'

In the small room behind the kitchen there was a smooth and sensual movement. Out came a handsome young woman, red as the queen of diamonds. She was tall and generous of build but moved with a springy lightness. Barelegged she was, the old brown shoes on her feet gaping across their cracked toe-creases, and she wore a tight yellow blouse and a flimsy rag of a green skirt. Her fleshy calves tapered swiftly to slim round ankles. She reminded Finney of an old painting he had seen somewhere, and she also reminded him strongly of his sister, Maryann, who had been a red-fleshed woman of very similar build.

'Get us a couple stouts,' Will ordered.

She met Finney's covering look and let her yellow eyes run over him as she turned back to the scullery. Her copper-coloured hair was moulded into a large mound on the back of her head above a long and tapered neck. Her sleevebands bit into the flesh of her upper arms like garters, while her bare forearms tapered to slim wrists and hands. She reminded him of every woman he had tumbled, and yet he had never seen her like before, nor could he remember what she looked like now that she was no longer before him.

Reading his puzzled appreciation, Will said, 'She's not a bad ould hure at all.' He carried a chair to the far corner of the hearth and sat to unlace a dirty boot. 'She keeps an eye on me. An ould man's nights are long an' lonely. But sit ye down, man! Draw up a chair an' tell us your travels.'

Finney moved slowly toward a chair, watching Will anxiously as the dog had done. He caught sight of his own face in a mirror and started. For a moment he thought it was himself he saw but younger, with a clear unbroken eye; but when he took a step closer to the glass, his reflection grew old once more.

'Take a chair, man!' Will demanded, crossing his legs to get at the lace.

Reluctantly Finney moved the chair to the opposite end of the hearth and sat. The fire was very hot. His damp coat and trousers steamed, warming the skin on his legs. He tried to think who this Peg could be. Will had never married. Someone had said that he had kept whores as housekeepers before . . . .

Will – dead? But he was nowhere near dead, sitting there, large, and dangerous as ever, after his usual Saturday spree. Finney decided that he must be getting mixed in his head: it was the effect of the fierce potheen and the fire. It could make a man drunk in several ways. But somehow he did not feel drunk now, and Will was seven-eighths drunk.

Will was lurching over the bootlace, saliva falling in little spider-webs from his mouth. 'Tell us about your travels, man,' he grumbled. He dropped his foot, boot and all, on the floor and swayed several times toward the fire, turning his head from the heat. Obediently, Finney searched his head, unable to find much worth the telling.

'Montreal it was,' he began. 'It was in Montreal, and I half-dead with the cold an' coughin' like a horse. I met up with a deck-hand who'd jumped ship to Liverpool. When I got there, the cops were waitin' for the guy whose name I had, but I slipped them since I looked nothin' like him, an' anyway, I had me own passport.'

Will still worked on the bootlace, his chair tipped forward on its front legs as he bent over. He was not listening. The savour of the boiling potatoes made Finney realize he was hungry. He had not had a feed like that for years.

'Go on!' said Will, absently.

'Then I came back home – yesterday, it was. Aye, yesterday. I guess that's about all,' he said shortly. It was as though he had sung for supper.

Then Peg slipped in with two glasses and four bottles of stout. She glanced contemptuously at Will's hunched form as she set them on the table. A swift and secret smile for Finney drifted across her lips. At high-breasted puberty with her long swan neck and sloping shoulders, Peg would have been like the young half-caste girl he had taken that time. Will might like to hear that.

'I noticed her in the town,' he said in a low voice. 'It was in Texas – near Houston. A green slip of a dress on her plump little body, an' I follered her out of the town in the dusk.'

Oddly, Will was not interested. He got rid of the first stubborn boot and glanced sideways at Peg and the bottles.

'Pull them for us,' he said.

She reached over across the table, opened and rummaged through a small drawer for a corkscrew. She could have handier moved round the table but leaned over and let her two breasts ride up out of the blouse. Finney stared, thinking how the young half-white's breasts had looked.

With an eye on its master, Will's dog arose and crept round the room by the walls to Peg and tried to lick her hand, but she ignored it.

Will's efforts with the second boot were very slow. The fire had made him drowsy, but when the stout gurgled in the glasses he reached a hand out sideways. Peg placed a glass in it, and brought the second one to Finney, standing in so close to him that her body brushed against his knees.

'Here's health, avic!' Will called, opening his mouth and slinging in the liquid.

Normally to Finney a bottle of stout was a good thing, but he did not want this one. He frowned casting about for a place to dump it. In the firelight it winked as red as blood, its foamy head like froth in a slaughterhouse drain. The thought sickened him.

Will stood the empty glass on the floor and carried on clumsily with the stubborn boot. Peg stood by the table fiddling with the corkscrew, forcing Finney to be aware of her, while the dog sat on its haunches under the table looking up. Absently, she slipped her left foot out of its shoe and scratched its belly. It caught at her leg with its canine mating grip, and she held out the leg to it.

Although all this pantomime seemed unaware and pointless, Finney knew it was for his benefit. It moved slighly the lust of his body but left him undisturbed. He wanted to be away. He had some place to go . . . .

'I have to go home, Will,' he said aloud. 'They'll be expecting me . . .' Neither Will nor Peg gave any sign they heard him.

'They . . . ?' he asked himself. Who were they? And then he had no home, never making one. No one was expecting him. No one even knew he was alive. He would get warm and dry at the fire and maybe get a feed of floury spuds and then get up and go. They could not hinder him.

Suddenly Peg spurned the dog, startling him, throwing it on to its back as though she had divined his indifference. She stared straight into his eyes. Her eyes were topaz-yellow, the firelight firing them as flames flickering, as knives flashing. Two hot hollows in her head they were, burning, but also dead. He met her eyes, pretending to plot with her, smiling and shaking his head quickly at the untouched stout in his hand, and she nodded understandingly.

Neatly, she picked Will's glass off the floor, just bending a knee slightly in her walk and lifting the glass in a single flowing motion as she came to Finney. She handed him the empty glass and took the full one, her hand reached above the rim and holding it close to her skirt as she passed back to the table behind Will.

'Haugh!' Will snorted, jerking back to life. 'Pull us another, Peg!'

'No, Will!' Finney protested. 'One's enough.'

'Arragh, not all, man!' Will insisted. 'Do ye good!'

Peg glanced from one to the other, the dog licking her anles.

'Pull him one!' Will ordered. He snapped the bootlace in irritation and dropped the boot to the floor. Finney felt the small taut pain of the snap in his chest, and Will spread his feet out in relief. Peg came to Finney for the empty glass.

'I've several hures of corns,' Will was complaining. 'Never get a bloody boot to fit me now.'

He wiggled his toes inside the socks, and then decided to take the right sock off, rolling it down from the elastic cuff of his white underpants and peeling it off.

Finney stared at the exposed foot. He could not see it properly but it seemed without flesh, the delicate bones and sinews without skin or cushioning muscle. When Will flexed the foot, the bones made the sound of turning pebbles. Finney felt sick, disbelieving his sight and blaming it. Men could not live and walk about on fleshless feet and next complain of corns; and Finney began to sweat.

'Aye – what about that little Jap callin' ye had in Chicago?' said Will, drawing the sock on again.

Finney sat up in surprise. He could not remember mentioning this girl (nor even the little Mexican girl in

39

San Pedro).

'She was a Filipino,' he corrected. 'I thought she was a Jap, but the papers said she was a Filipino. I followed her down the street. A cop was coming up and I waited by a burned-out house. She came back with groceries and suckin' an ice-cream. There was an El going past at the time. She wasn't a Jap. She was a Filipino . . . .'

'No matter, no matter,' said Will contentedly. 'Put their heads in a bag, an' they all look alike, avic.'

Finney chuckled. He kept seeing the olive face of the girl.

'I didn't hurt her,' he explained. 'I did it like the guy in the movies. Don't be blamin' me, Will. I – I was terrible lonely, so I just tried to live my own way.'

Will was staring into the fire, and Finney could not say if he was listening or not. He glanced at Peg. The changing firelight made her face ovoid and lean and gave her the features of the Filipino girl. Smiling, she turned to the table.

Pop went the corks, the sharp sounds jarring Finney to the depths of his body. As if alive, the stout spewed from the bottle necks. With her right hand Peg filled the empty glass and drank Finney's from her left, then filled and delivered two full glasses. As she returned past Will, the old man reached for her roughly.

Looking into Finney's eyes, she gave to his pull, and Finney felt ashamed for Will and the woman, even for himself. He knew Will wanted to name the woman, to boast about her and condemn her. And all the while Will's arm was tightening around her, pulling her against him. Her eyes never left Finney's face, and the dog crept out from under the table, wagging its tail and whining.

'She's not a bad old hure, is Peg,' said Will.

His fingers haunched a handful of the skirt and

skin on her belly and she winced.

'Washes, darns, cooks . . . . ' He laughed.

Inwardly disgusted, Finney forced himself to snicker, and the dog heard and came over to look into his face. He wanted to get up but was powerless to leave his chair. His blood seemed set on fire. It surged through his body in sickening waves.

'She's a good traveller, bigod,' Will was saying, and Finney pressed back against the chair to steady himself.

He had never had such a sensation of lightness, and had to hold himself down by hooking a hand under the chair. In so doing, the glass of stout in his left hand tipped, and some of the liquid spilled on to his knee where it made an ice-cold patch. He took a mouthful but could not swallow it, holding it in his mouth and swilling it round his teeth until it grew warm and salty as blood. Will and the woman were now in grotesque embrace.

'Hegh, hegh, hegh!' Will laughed.

'I want to go,' Finney tried to say. 'I must get away.'

'By God, she can carry me!' Will crowed. 'Can't ye, Peg, asthore?'

Peg smiled a demure cat smile, self-satisfied as a purr. Her empty yellow eyes had blazed at Finney the entire time, and he thought, 'She has something to tell me. That's why she watches me.'

'Look ye, avic!' Will bawled. 'She has the best backside in the country!'

He dropped his free hand, gathering the skirt into his fist and hoisting it. But it was the cruelty of the hand as it lay upon the fire-touched softness of the woman's belly that fascinated Finney. The hand was now a claw and, as the foot had been, fleshless and hard as a hawk's talon. Then the skirt fell back as Peg pivoted suddenly and moved away, and Will roared

41

in senseless laughter.

His laughter rippled the thickening air like the shatter of a stone in a pool, and Finney peered across the fire at the two of them as though through the opacity of water. Still laughing, Will threw down the second glass of stout. First he spluttered, then erupted in a gasping spasm that forced the liquid through his nostrils and down over his chin. He coughed and snorted, his hands fluttering in the watery air like a drowning man.

Unmoved, Peg stood by the table, the excited dog cowering by her feet. Finney felt vaguely sorry for her while knowing she did not need nor ask for pity.

'Pouff!' Will cried. His wind at least was back, and he was shaking his head. Peg's eyes moved slowly over him. The room was quiet now, and the lid on the pot of potatoes gave a single dying sigh.

Although his front was scorched, Finney's back was chill, the fire's convection drawing the cold air off the night. He looked up, and there seemed no top to the house. There was snow drifting past, caught momentarily in the light.

'Why don't ye go to bed, Will?' Peg advised. She came over for Will's empty glass and whipped Finney's away as before.

'Whaaaa?' said Will, looking craftily at Finney.

Peg shrugged. Pushing three fingers and the thumb of her right hand into the necks of the empty bottles, and nipping the full and empty glasses together with her left hand, she glided into the scullery. Finney heard the squeal, groan and suck of a pump as she rinsed the glasses.

Will settled himself in his chair, muttering and frowning.

Finney cleared his throat and said as firmly as he dared, 'I have to be going now, Will.'

'Whaaaa?' Will asked. 'Haugh!' he snorted, under-standing. 'Time enough, man! There's allus enough time for everything.'

A log rolled off another's burning back in a pretty shower of sparks, darkening the hearth. The light's new illusion made Will appear as a full skeleton. His domed head teetered on the neck column, and his jaw fixed itself to an awful permanent grin. Finney shuddered, trying to make the sign of the cross, and Will called absently, 'Peg? Make up the fire.'

She came over from the scullery door and kneeled down on the hearth, beautiful now in the diffused light, taking a pair of tongs with delicate queenly gesture and re-laying the fire's cone, building in some new logs and carefully picking up each little red eye of charcoal.

The collie rose, stretched, cocked its leg against the table leg, and came over to Finney, snuggling its stone-cold nose into his left hand, then going over lazily to Peg.

It stood by her shoulder. She was reclining, leaning on her left arm facing the fire, her breasts leaning one on the other to her left side, her right hand inert on her right thigh, so still and relaxed that the fire's false flames made her at once small and large, visible and invisible, a torso that rested one moment in the earth and the very next disclosed a shadowed, rounded form without humanity. The dog tried to lick her face, and the fire said she was a dog-headed being cut on a shadow-frieze and as old as time.

She moved her head and pushed the beast away with her right hand, then fondled and teased it absently at arm's length.

Will stared unblinkingly into the fire, and he hummed, 'I tore me ould britches goin' over the ditches to you, Maryann, to you, Maryann . . .'

43

It was an old folk ditty that Finney had heard as a boy. It had a light lilting tune. 'What's the rest of that, Will?' he asked.

There was no reply as Will stared on into the fire. The dog lay now with its head on Peg's thigh. The big pot was boiling dry, and an unpleasant smell was beginning to fill the room.

Behind Will there came another woman, an aborigine and brown almost to blackness with dark and bestially yearning eyes and two strong scars or caste marks cut into each cheek on either side of the broad flat nose and two rows of beadlike scars across her chest above the roots of her low leathery breasts. Her hands were held behind her back. She was quite naked and seemed young. She moved closer to the old man, looking down on his head with a terrible intensity of inarticulate love, and fear, and pity. Will seemed to sense her presence and shrugged uncomfortably, glancing unwillingly to the side.

'Peg?' he muttered, putting out a hand to feel for her.

The hand moved in an arc through the aborigine's body, his eyes following the gesture into their corners so that his bloodshot bulging grey eyeballs filled their sockets like one who was quite sightless or was dead.

Shuddering violently, he said, 'Haugh!' and Peg broke into a brazen trill of a laugh that raced round the room and fled outside to join the wind's wild laughter.

'Quiet!' Will roared.

'Go to bed!' she chided.

'Aye,' he muttered, crestfallen. 'Aye, bed . . . .'

The dog went to him and whined, sniffing round the dark woman's bare feet. Will cursed at it, his eyes refusing to look sideways. With bowed head the native woman went away, and her hands were tied

44

with rope behind her back, the crease of the backbone and the two mounds of the shoulder bones stamped momentarily by the fire magic into the form of a cross. Finney chuckled hysterially, thinking about an ass.

'The cross of an ass,' he said aloud. 'Steal the cross off an ass . . . .'

It was a country saying to denote a real rogue. Scraps of religion Finney had learned and discarded were coming back to him – the great ride on the ass up to the city, then the spittle and the tied hands, Peter cowering by the fire saying 'No, no' in his long Jewish shirt like Maryann crying by the fire.

With a brief flicker of life Will sat up and stretched. He looked over at Finney.

Embarrassed and scared, Finney said, 'Tell us the rest of Maryann, Will?'

'Maryann she want a man, her babby needs a daddio!'

'No!' Finney shouted. 'No no!'

Peg laughed wildly again, opening her mouth, her red tongue bunched behind her white lower teeth.

'Oh, husha – husha!' Will complained, shaking his head. 'This is a most distressful country, man! The dear ould shamrock's lawless, now. Have ye seen Tandy?'

'Tandy?' Finney asked.

Peg started to sing softly into the fire: 'I'ee met wid Napper Tandy an' I tuk him be the han' now tell me how is Ire-lan' an' how diz she stan' . . . .' Will dropped his chin on his chest and smiled contentedly. Peg forgot the words and hummed the verse out.

The burned pot was now making black snakes of smoke that writhed and curled like ropes round the room, binding the three of them together in a stinking web. The smell made Finney want to vomit.

Will was remembering:

45

'Maryann she found the man
to dance upon her diddio
And got a father for her bairn,
her pore wee laddio.'

'Go to bed!' Peg said impatiently.

'I'll be going,' Finney said. He was feigning nonchalance and trying but failing to rise, as though the sour smoke ropes now bound him to his seat. There was a dull moist pounding pain in his chest; and he pressed his back against the chair to lean away from it.

Will grunted, nodding, and stiffly rose to his feet. Peg got to her knees on the hearth, unnecessarily putting her two hands on Finney's knees to assist her rising.

'Do ye want anythin' to ate, Will?' she asked with a smirk.

'No,' he said, shaking his head. 'The dead can't enjoy their food an' their board is allus empty. They may on'y sleep. Quiet sleep does be a good thing.'

He yawned, rubbing a numb hand over his thick-thatched grey head and, peering down on Finney, asked suspiciously, 'What's he doin' here?'

'Who?' Peg asked.

'Oh,' he said secretly, 'I thought I saw somethin'. I keep thinkin' I see things about me. I keep drinkin' pints I swallowed long ago. In the town this day I saw a tall fair woman, but a pickle of corn formed her mouth an' her two diddies slapped together like clappers fit to fright crows. Aye . . . .'

He lumbered to the door, domestically undoing his vest and top fly buttons and yawning. Opening the door, he peered out and urinated over the threshold into the night. A coldness came into the room, a solid ice-block of tangible cold the same shape and size as the door. Outside there was darkness with snow-flowers dropping through the oblong of light. The falling snow reminded Finney of something he should tell Will.

'I was sheltering in an office doorway,' he whispered. 'The snow was thick in the air. Thousands of people were coming out of work an' hurrying into the snow with their heads down. Goin' home, they were, to warm bright places. A girl in a white mackintosh came past me. She stood on the step an' complained about the snow. Then she turned and smiled at me before she went off. I followed her. She cut across the park. The park was a quiet wilderness of snow, but she screamed when I caught her an' a big cop came runnin'.

'Where's the wind from?' Peg called, her back to the fire and her two open hands with the backs to her behind to keep the heat off.

'Wind?' Will asked. 'No wind,' he said, looking around, 'just snow fallin'. No wind mor'n the sigh of a worm in the soil . . .'

'Oh,' Peg said. 'It must be somebody cryin' in the night I heard.

Will closed the door, but the snow continued to fall into the room now, hissing into the fire with small swift secret hisses and the fire was afraid now of dying and caught the flakes with hot anger. He came slowly across the room, muttering, a sprinkling of snow on his head and shoulders. 'Not a bad night – not a bad night at all for to die.'

'Die?' Finney whispered. 'Who said anythin' 'bout dyin', man? Chrisake, let me outa here!'

'Don't let him moider ye,' Peg advised kindly. 'He does think deep things in his age. The world is allus full of wild words an' sleep, avic. Go to bed, Will? Go to bed an' say your prayers.'

'I mind – I mind the time when the whole wide world was a wildflower of goold in me hand,' he said hesitatingly and sadly. 'I mind – I mind the cailíns skippin' along the roads. People moved with a dance in their legs them days . . .'

'Husha, now!' Peg scolded, taking his heavy right arm and turning him to face the steep stairs. 'It's the wooden hills an' blanket valleys for ye, avic!'

'This wide world's a broken pore place now,' Will said. 'An ould bedstead wid rusty springs . . . aye. Bed for the gettin', bed for the birthin', an' bed for the dyin' away . . .'

'Oh, husha, husha!' Peg said again, shaking his arm. 'Ye'd jaw the crow off the corncock! Bed an' prayers!'

'Aye, bed an' prayers,' Will said forlornly, 'the bread an' butter of life . . .'

On weighted feet he moved to the stairs, starting in a hopeful, childish treble to say, 'Now, I lay me down to sleep, I pray the Lord me soul to keep . . .'

Peg came back and lifted the lamp off the wall and followed him, the light fanning mysteriously about her face, casting small shadows off its contours into its hollows and making her Mary meek and beautiful. With slow creaking steps Will climbed, his feet dropping on each step like stones, and ahead of him Finney could see no end to the long stairway as though it slanted into space and rode up into the lost darkness of the night. '. . . wake I at morn or wake I never . . .'

On the floor above, their feet pounded and shuffled as though they were making heavy songless dance, the wind now a single nervous note on a single string seeking like a whining dog around the house. The collie dog came over to Finney and lay down by his feet for company.

48

Without the lamp the fire failed to master the shadows which took possession of the kitchen up to the hot edge of the hearthstone, and Finney watched the light and shadow warriors writhe in silent struggle – cowering, crouching, leaping, lunging.

The pot was making as much fume as a factory chimney, and he gasped labouring for a clean reath, the bulbous cords of smoke twisting about the room.

He tried to move off the chair by putting his weight on his arms. When he stood with great effort, the floor reeled like the deck of a boat. 'Home now,' he thought, 'the black backs of the Donegal hills on the dawn sky.'

Against Will's mumbling prayers Peg started to sing: 'They dressed me up in scarlet red an' treated me very kindly but I could not forget the girl that I'ee left behin' me . . .'

'Quiet!' Will roared like a blow. 'Quiet, ye blasphemous bitch!'

Although his body ran with sweat, Finney tucked by habit the lapels of his coat under his chin. The talk and fumbling upstairs had ceased, and the bed complained as Will lay down on it, and then Peg laughed her high wild laugh. So wild was it that it might have been a blast of wind across the chimney, and the dog lifted its head and gave a long wailing call that sent a shiver down Finney's back.

'Where – where am I at all?' he whispered, gazing around and seeing the room now with a white snow layer over everything.

Fixing his eyes on the distant door, he moved slowly towards it and had a hand on the latch when he heard Peg's voice softly behind him.

'Ye're not goin'?' she asked as though surprised.

He could just barely see her outline against the fire's decreasing cone, her hands on her hips, her elbows sticking out like jug handles. He moved his thick tongue over his lips.

'Ye're not feered of me?' she challenged.

'No,' he whispered.

'What ails ye, then?'

He did not know what to say.

'This night is young an' quiet as t'grave now,' she said like a purr, glancing sideways at the stairs. 'Come on – if ye're a man at all!'

She lifted the hem of her skirt above her knees, moving her body in a poor gesture of allurement, offering herself as women across the world offered themselves to men one way or another. The old broken shoes slapping up and down on her heels, she made a little dance and sang: 'O lovely Maryann! Me gentle little swan! Where'er I bee I'll dream of thee, till life's last pulse is gone . . .'

'Shut up!' he said, choking. 'Ye're a witch – a bloody witch! A witch is what ye are! A witch . . .' He kept saying witch, unable to stop.

Peg laughed, and the dog came to her, whining and wagging its tail. She held out her foot to it, balancing on the right one and teasing it as she had done before.

'I'm sick,' Finney complained. She was playing a clever game, and he saw through it. If he started on her she would kill him. 'I'd – I'd be no good to ye,' he muttered in mock shame. She laughed in her throat, richly and proudly, flinging the dog away.

Upstairs in a dream Will shouted, 'Haugh!' the bed creaking like a wind-tormented door. 'Git t'hell away from me!' he roared. 'Bygone is bygone – let t'dead bury t'dead for God's sake!'

'Ye wouldn't be feered of the pore old man?' she asked, innocently.

Taking his hand off the latch, he turned back. 'Tell me, is he dead?' he said.

She gave her wild loud laugh, throwing back her

head and opening her mouth.

'Stop laughin' at me!' he shouted, the strength of his shout starting a cough deep in his throat, and blood came to the corners of his mouth. She waited politely till he ceased, and said slowly:

'What is death? Everything lives for the dead an' the deeds of the living are the food of the dead an' dead men are free fancy men, no bargain binds them. They sing in their dreams an' live in the morrow. Come – don't be freckened.'

She reached forward gently and took his left arm, leading him over to the fire across the snow-powdered floor. She kneeled on the hearth, drawing him down beside her, saying softly, 'Ah musha, musha – a fire is a grand thing . . .'

They watched the fire. it was dying, the heavy snow-flakes sizzling on the red-bright logs and freckling the mass with black dead stains. 'The snow'sa killin' the fire,' Peg said, sadly. 'I've often wondered where fire does be when it dies. Fire's a quare thing . . .'

She held his right hand firmly and comfortingly in her left. 'I've waited the long time till ye come back. I never forgot . . .'

She turned her body to him, putting her two hands on his shoulders and pushing him down so he was flat on the hearth. Kneeling beside him, she pushed the dog away when it scrabbled across his body and tried to lick her face. Leaning over him, she grasped his wrists and lifted them above his head, pinning them to the floor, pressing her heavy weight of breast upon his chest. 'The dog kept moving round them. 'Lew' she commanded. 'Lew – lie down!'

'No – no!' Finney wheezed, unable to draw a full breath with the weight of her. With a great effort he wrenched free his hands and tried to push her away.

He could not move her and for an eternity he tensed his body against her, sweating and panting and whispering: 'No! No! No! No!'

Upstairs the bed squeaked and they heard a gurgling cough. The bed creaked loudly again, and a heavy form blundered on to the floor along with the musical shattering of glass. The dog sat on its haunches and started a low long tenor yowl in its throat rising and falling in a minor key . . . .

Finney was puzzled. Peg's body was not soft. It was hard – hard and heavy as a boulder crushing down on him. In a wild rage he grasped at her breasts and they were cold and soft as snow. He buried his fingers in them, filling his fists with them and the handfuls came away, the flesh white and cold like snow, and the dog, barking sharply now, started tugging at his sleeve.

Peg's face still wore a smile – not a triumphant nor a satisfied smile: an ancient, motiveless, sexless smile unanswerable and unceasing. Gathering his strength he flung her away, craving every breath but scared to draw the air too deeply. He shut his eyes and concentrated on the breathing, jealously feeding the air in little mouthfuls into his aching lungs.

When he opened his eyes the whole room was white and the fire had gone out, the dog still shivering and whining beside him. Then he saw Will standing on the bottom step of the stairs in what seemed a long white nightshirt, his face grey and vacant and calm.

Finney was dead scared now. Will could kill him. 'No – no,' he whispered, cowering down on the floor beside the dog. Will paid no attention and walked over to the door which swung open before him, letting in a clear cool wind that churned up the choking smoke rings and blew them away.

To Finney the room now seemed wall-less as a sea,

a white sea without bound or border. He stood up, his weariness gone. Will was standing with his right hand upraised in a sign of benediction and acceptance, and then he beckoned with the left hand.

'Will . . .?' Finney whispered, not sure whether the figure was Will or not.

Then, looking down on the dog, he moved away from it without effort, a great lightness in him, and he knew he was free at last to leave earth, earthlust, lifelust and lust behind. Swiftly he followed the white figure out into the vast coenobium of the night that listened to the song of the church bells carolling for Christmas Day . . . .

The Christmas morning a neighbour who had been at Bob Dowden's card party told the Poyntzes that Adam was back in the old country and acting like a millionaire. Maryann took the news quietly – it seemed little more than a waking day continuation of a dream she had had the night before about her brother and herself in childhood: one of a thousand dreams, the old event unburied and working through the lagan of her soul.

The children were stirred, the vagueness round their uncle's existence clothing him in a heroic glamour. Poyntz was in short humour. The snow had slowed his morning chores. They were all likely to be late for Church. He was a one thing at a time man and small crises always upset him.

He bundled the harness on the cob and led it to the trap, calling: 'Hasten, there! Hasten, now!' impatiently nibbling his lower lip with its tiny goatbeard of grey hair as they climbed in, and driving off before they were settled.

The children were wide-eyed at the blizzard's transformation of the old green land, its cracks and scars healed by a salve of snow, each aching angle filled with a fillet of snow, the tree boles rinded with snow, their leafless branches pointing to the pale-blue sun-bright sky: snow was a seldom thing and when it came so well it was a miracle.

Maryann said nothing, holding her last baby in her arms, looking with inscrutable gaze at the plain craggy features of her husband, a man full forty years her senior, and wondering about her brother.

The cob made its own pace on the slippery road, it refused to hasten and Poyntz was nervous it might go down. He kept clicking his tongue and fussing with the reins, trying to pick rough patches in the road ahead and denying the cob the full use of its own wisdom. The church bell began to ring. It would ring for twenty minutes and to be in time they should have passed Knock Crossroads and not be a half-mile below it. Poyntz could see the church spire's black finger across the white fields and fretted, nibbling his lips. He was strict about church matters and would sooner turn back from the door than disturb a service.

The snow hurt his dull eyes and he was weary after a heavy morning's work shovelling the drifts round the buildings. At Templemore overhanging trees had kept the snow soft and the cob was able to trot. Then young John shouted, startling them all:

'Daddo! Daddo! There's a dog! We've passed a black shepherd dog, daddo!'

Maryann and young Mary followed the boy's imperious pointing.

Poyntz scowled, not looking around and muttering: 'Never mind! never mind!'

'It's on a rope, daddo! It's tied to a rope!'

Poyntz glanced at his wife, who nodded agreement with the boy, but he said, shrugging distastefully: 'Leave it be! We're late as it is!'

'But it's tied to somethin', daddo!' the boy protested

tearfully. 'It's caught! Let me go get it. You go on an I'll catch ye.'

'Be still or ye'll toss the cob!' Poyntz ordered, but knowing his mother was with him, the boy had already flung off the rug and was clambering over the trap-door. The shifting weight upset the cob and it slid nervously to a halt.

'Whoa!' Poyntz cried helplessly. 'Stay where ye are, damn it!'

But young John was away down the road, clots of snow flying over his back.

The little bitch whined gladly, leaning on the rope and trying to lick his hand, her thin body a constant shiver.

'Good bitch – good bitch,' he encouraged softly, putting a hand on her head and running his fingers down the frost-stiff rope and then pulling on the rope to free it and lifting up what looked like a gnarled bit of a branch.

But it was not a branch, and although unwilling to accept his eyes' evidence the boy saw a grey human hand in a sleeve clawed round a small pellet of pink snow, a grey hand on a wood-stiff wrist and a coral egg of frozen snow in it, pink snow like the icing on his mother's Christmas cake . . . .

He dropped the rope and the hand dropped back. His eyes swiftly measured the dimensions of the snowy mound, the awful mound soiled and trampled by the dog's restless paws.

A long way off they were waiting in the trap – watching from the trap a thousand miles away, his father beckoning impatiently. He tried to shout but his voice only made a whisper. The dog licked his bare knees. He waved with both arms and heard his father ask: 'What hell's wrong wid him?'

The boy pointed to the ground and waved again.

Maryann turned back the rug, opened the trap-door and got out. The boy saw her actions with a relief he would never forget; her coming to him down the road on the soft snow verge, the baby in her arms, her breath making little clouds about her head, a dead oak beyond her with crooked fingers crying to the sky: he could hardly wait and yet remain alive . . . . Oh, hasten, hasten.

When she was near he whispered, 'It's a man, ma?' asking her if she knew and hoping he was wrong. 'The dog's tied to it . . .'

Maryann stood above the mound, her bright frost-fired face going sallow. 'God save us,' she whispered, looking down into her son's eyes. 'Some poor man got caught in the storm,' she added protectively against the boy's terror, his fear-opened features shocking her they looked so like his uncle's.

'Get daddo,' he was saying hoarsely.

In the trap Poyntz chewed his lower lip, acutely conscious of the hurrying bell, but in answer to his wife's summons he climbed out and went to the cob's head, telling the Mary child to hold the reins as he turned the animal and led it back, calling crossly: 'What hell's up – we're surely late now!'

When he saw the hand and the mound he removed his hard hat, his white bald head waxen in the sun. He was shocked, but said practically: 'Don't stir anythin'. We'll have to tell the police.'

But John refused to leave the dog behind: no more than he could stay there himself could he leave the dog nor bear to think and think of it being there nightlong, nightlong tethered to a dead man's hand . . . .

Poyntz could not bring himself to touch the hand and slip the *dul* off the wrist, so he cut the noose from the dog's neck. He was curious about the man but did not want to remove the shroud of snow before the children . . . .

'What is it?' Mary called from the trap.

'Nothin' – nothin',' he grumbled, nodding to wife and son to come away and frightened in himself – five years beyond the Abrahamic span, a death diminished his own slow-running sand.

John lifted the bitch, sobbing in his chest with pity and shock. They put it in the warm well of the trap between their legs under the rug and started off again.

'We can call the po-lice from t'Rect'ry,' Poyntz said, still thinking about church although the service would be half over when they got that far.

Maryann watched her son and to soothe his mind said conversationally: 'That's old Will Curry's place.'

They all glanced at the roofless house and tumbled steadings, their gaunt starkness trebled by the bland snow's perfection.

The baby started to cry, singing ah-lah, ah-lah, ah-lah and kicking with each syllable. Maryann shushed it and started to undo her coat, fumbling in her blouse for a breast and clamping the child's face against it and holding it there, her hand palmed over the back of its baby-bald head. It sucked strongly and guttered in its napkin. Young John heard it and thought how bothersome babies were. He could feel the great nervous shudders of the bitch against his legs. They could all feel the shudders moving coldly through their bodies.

'Will Uncle Adam be at the church?' Mary asked.

'We'll see,' Maryann replied shortly.

'It's odd he didn't come over,' Poyntz said as though the idea had just struck him. Maryann did not reply.

She fed the child and watched her boy, seeing afresh the great likeness to his uncle. He was fourteen now, although he looked and acted more like ten, a gentle quiet lad with little sign of wildness. Oh, she watched him closely for any sign of wildness, and the neighbours kept saying: My, oh my, is he not the pure Finney!

Well, why not – since he was pure Finney. No one knew that and no one would ever know.

The church bell had stopped for five minutes before Poyntz heard the silence of it. He glanced at his wife and saw a strange woman with hard tawny eyes in a set stony face. Had he been able to see in the dark her expression would have been familiar, but this was the first time she had betrayed it in daylight.

She was looking at him, through him, past him, mercilessly unseeing him as a man at all, neither as husband nor as human being; seeing a toothless old hag-hulk of a man, guileful and gullible, an old goat-lusty bag-o'-bones bald man . . . . But she did not hate him at all, she only despised him while fond of him in an odd way, and could thole him as many a woman bore with many a man, many a worse or better man, good or bad making little difference: and Poyntz was much like a boy now, his fumbling passion swift and shy as a boy's.

No – hate she reserved for her brother Adam, a cold glazed time-fired stone of hate lying secretly in her heart for his witless useless action, sin neither here nor there, that had given her for once the pain of pleasure and the pleasure of terror on a drunken lawless whim, and then condemned her to a slow life of frustration alongside an old man with age-old, age-flabby skin, day eking day, night borrowing night, dream denying dream. She looked at her son, praying a desperate secret prayer, asking that he should not be wild or queer, that she should learn to love him less, but never learn to hate him as she lived lonely in the ritual prison of her regret.

58

Concentrating on the ground ahead of the cob's forefeet, Poyntz asked, 'What's wrong?'

After a silence she answered untruthfully but with more truthfulness than she divined: 'I was thinkin' about that pore man . . . .'

Young John slipped a hand down under the rug and touched the bitch's wet head and felt the grateful tongue licking him. He could still see the snow-enbalmed hand, a grey talon jessed to the shivering dog fawning in utter gratitude before him, the autochthonous hand raising itself out of the snow. Come Christmas with or without snow, come snow in January or in May, he would always see the hand and feel the heaviness of it on a frozen rope . . . .

TWO OF A KIND

SEAN O'FAOLAIN

Maxer Creedon was not drunk, but he was melancholy-drunk, and he knew it and he was afraid of it.

At first he had loved being there in the jammed streets, with everybody who passed him carrying parcels wrapped in green or gold, tied with big red ribbons and fixed with berried holly sprigs. Whenever he bumped into someone, parcels toppled and they both cried 'Ooops!' or 'Sorree!' and laughed at one another. A star of snow sank nestling into a woman's hair. He smelled pine and balsam. He saw twelve golden angels blaring silently from twelve golden trumpets in Rockefeller Plaza. He pointed out to a cop that when the traffic lights down Park Avenue changed from red to green the row of Christmas trees away down the line changed colour by reflection. The cop was very grateful to him. The haze of light on the tops of the buildings made a halo over Fifth Avenue. It was all just the way he knew it would be, and he slopping down from Halifax in that damned old tanker. Then, suddenly, he swung his right arm in a wild arc of disgust.

'To hell with 'em! To hell with everybody!'

'Oops! Hoho, there! Sorree!'

He refused to laugh back.

'Poor Creedon!' he said to himself. 'All alone in New York, on Christmas-bloody-well-Eve, with nobody to talk to, and nowhere to go only back to the bloody old ship. New York all lit up. Everybody all lit up. Except poor old Creedon.'

He began to cry for poor old Creedon. Crying, he reeled through the passing feet. The next thing he knew he was sitting up at the counter of an Eighth Avenue drugstore sucking black coffee, with one eye screwed-up to look out at the changing traffic lights, chuckling happily over a yarn his mother used to tell him long ago about a place called Ballyroche. He had been there only once, nine years ago, for her funeral. Beaming into his coffee cup, or looking out at the changing traffic lights, he went through his favourite yarn about Poor Lily:

'Ah, wisha! Poor Lily! I wonder where is she atall atall now. Or she dead or alive. It all happened through an Italian who used to be going from one farm to another selling painted statues. Bandello his name was, a handsome black divil ' hell! I never in all my born days saw a more handsome divil. Well, one wet, wild windy October morning what did she do but creep out of her bed and we all sound asleep and go off with him. Often and often I heard my father say that the last seen of her was standing under the big tree at Ballyroche Cross, sheltering from the rain, at about eight o'clock in the morning. It was Mikey Clancy the postman saw her. "Yerrah, Lily girl," says he, "what are you doing here at this hour of the morning?" "I'm waiting," says she, "for to go into Fareens on the milk cart." And from that day to this not a sight nor a sound of her no more than if the earth had swallowed her. Except for the one letter from a priest in America to say she was happily married in Brooklyn, New York.'

Maxer chuckled again. The yarn always ended up with the count of the years. The last time he heard it the count had reached forty-one. By this year it would have been fifty.

61

Maxer put down his cup. For the first time in his life it came to him that the yarn was a true story about a real woman. For as long as four traffic-light changes he fumbled with this fact. Then, like a man hearing a fog signal come again and again from an approaching ship, and at last hearing it close at hand, and then seeing an actual if dim shape, wrapped in a coccoon of haze, the great idea revealed itself.

He lumbered down from his stool and went over to the telephones. His lumpish finger began to trace its way down the grey pages among the Brooklyn's *Ban's*. His finger stopped. He read the name aloud. *Bandello, Mrs Lily*. He found a dime, tinkled it home, and dialled the number slowly. On the third ring he heard an old woman's voice. Knowing that she would be very old and might be deaf, he said very loudly and with the extra-meticulous enunciation of all drunks:

'My name is Matthew Creedon. Only my friends call me Maxer. I come from Limerick, Ireland. My mother came from the townland of Ballyroche. Are you by any chance my Auntie Lily?'

Her reply was a bark:

'What do you want?'

'Nothing at all! Only I thought, if you are the lady in question, that we might have a bit of an ould gosther. I'm a sailor. Docked this morning in the Hudson.

The voice was still hard and cold:

'Did somebody tell you to call me?'

He began to get cross with her.

'Naw! Just by a fluke I happened to look up your name in the directory. I often heard my mother talking about you. I just felt I'd like to talk to somebody. Being Christmas and all that. And knowing nobody in New York. But if you don't like the idea, it's okay with me. I don't want to butt in on anybody. Good-bye.'

'Wait! You're sure nobody sent you?'

'Inspiration sent me! Father Christmas sent me!'
(She could take that any way she bloody-well liked!)
'Look! It seems to me I'm buttin' in. Let's skip it.'

'No. Why don't you come over and see me?'

Suspiciously he said:

'This minute?'

'Right away!'

At the sudden welcome of her voice all his
annoyance vanished.

'Sure, Auntie Lily! I'll be right over. But, listen, I
sincerely hope you're not thinking I'm buttin' in.
Because if you are . . .'

'It was very nice of you to call me, Matty, very nice
indeed. I'll be glad to see you.'

He hung up, grinning. She was just like his mother
– the same old Limerick accent. After fifty years. And
the same bossy voice. If she was a day she'd be
seventy. She'd be tall, and thin, and handsome, and
the real lawdy-daw, doing the grand lady, and under
it all she'd be as soft as mountain moss. She'd be
tidying the house now like a divil. And giving jaw to
ould Bandello. If he was still alive.

He got lost on the subway, so that when he came up
it was dark. He paused to have another black coffee.
Then he paused to buy a bottle of Jamaica rum as a
present for her. And then he had to walk five blocks
before he found the house where she lived. The
automobiles parked under the lights were all snow-
covered. She lived in a brown-stone house with high
steps. Six other families also had rooms in it.

The minute he saw her on top of the not brightly lit
landing, looking down at him, he saw something he
had completely forgotten. She had his mother's
height, and slimness, and her wide mouth, but he had
forgotten the pale, liquid blue of the eyes and they
stopped him dead on the stairs, his hand tight on the

banister. At the sight of them he heard the soft wind sighing over the level Limerick plain and his whole body shivered. For miles and miles not a sound but that soughing wind that makes the meadows and the wheat fields flow like water. All over that plain, where a cross-roads is an event, where a little, sleepy lake is an excitement. Where their streams are rivers to them. Where their villages are towns. The resting cows look at you out of owls' eyes over the greasy tips of the buttercups. The meadow grass is up to their bellies. Those two pale eyes looking down at him were bits of the pale albino sky stretched tightly over the Shannon plain.

Slowly he climbed up to meet her, but even when they stood side by side she was still able to look down at him, searching his face with her pallid eyes. He knew what she was looking for, and he knew she had found it when she threw her bony arms around his neck and broke into a low, soft wailing just like that Shannon wind.

'Auntie! You're the living image of her!'

On the click of a finger she became bossy and cross with him, hauling him by his two hands into her room:

'You've been drinking! And what delayed you? And I suppose not a scrap of solid food in your stomach since morning?'

He smiled humbly.

'I'm sorry, Auntie. 'Twas just on account of being all alone, you know. And everybody else making whoopee.' He hauled out the peace offering of the rum. 'Let's have a drink!'

She was fussing all over him immediately.

'You gotta eat something first. Drinking like that all day, I'm ashamed of you! Sit down, boy. Take off your jacket. I got coffee, and cookies, and hamburgers, and

64

a pie. I always lay in a stock for Christmas. All of the neighbours visit me. Everybody knows that Lily Bandello keeps an open house for Christmas, nobody is ever going to say Lily Bandello didn't have a welcome for all her friends and relations at Christmas-time . . .'

She bustled in and out of the kitchenette, talking back to him without stop.

It was a big, dusky room, himself looking at himself out of the tall mirrored wardrobe piled on top with cardboard boxes. There was a divan in one corner as high as a bed, and he guessed that there was a washbasin behind the old peacock-screen. A single bulb hung in the centre of the ceiling, in a fluted glass bell with pink frilly edges. The pope over the bed was Leo XIII. The snowflakes kept touching the bare windowpanes like kittens' paws trying to get in. When she began on the questions, he wished he had not come.

'How's Bid?' she called out from the kitchen.

'Bid? My mother? Oh, well, of course, I mean to say . . . My mother? Oh, she's grand, Auntie! Never better. For her age, of course, that is. Fine, fine out! Just like yourself. Only for the touch of old rheumatism now and again.'

'Go on, tell me about all of them. How's Uncle Matty? And how's Cis? When were you down in Ballyroche last? But, sure, it's all changed now I suppose, with electric light and everything up to date? And I suppose the old pony and trap is gone years ago? It was only last night I was thinking of Mikey Clancey the postman.' She came in, planking down the plates, an iced Christmas cake, the coffeepot. 'Go on! You're telling me nothing.'

She stood over him, waiting, her pale eyes wide, her mouth stretched. He said:

'My Uncle Matty? Oh well, of course, now he's not as young as he was. But I saw him there last year. He was looking fine. Fine out. I'd be inclined to say he'd be a bit stooped. But in great form. For his age, that is.'

'Sit in. Eat up. Eat up. Don't mind me. He has a big family now, no doubt?'

'A family? Naturally! There's Tom. And there's Kitty, that's my Aunt Kitty, it *is* Kitty, isn't it, yes, my Aunt Kitty. And . . . God, I can't remember the half of them.'

She shoved the hamburgers towards him. She made him pour the coffee and tell her if he liked it. She told him he was a bad reporter.

'Tell me all about the old place!'

He stuffed his mouth to give him time to think.

'They have twenty-one cows. Holsteins. The black and white chaps. And a red barn. And a shelter belt of pines. 'Tis lovely there now to see the wind in the trees, and when the night falls the way the lighthouse starts winking at you, and . . .'

'What lighthouse?' She glared at him. She drew back from him. 'Are ye daft? What are you dreaming about? Is it a lighthouse in the middle of the County Limerick?'

'There is a lighthouse! I saw it in the harbour!'

But he suddenly remembered that where he had seen it was in a toyshop on Eighth Avenue, with a farm beyond it and a red barn and small cows, and a train going round and round it all.

'Harbour, Matty? Are ye out of your senses?'

'I saw it with my own two eyes.'

His eyes were like marbles. Suddenly she leaned over like a willow – just the way his mother used to lean over – and laughed and laughed.

'I know what you're talking about now. The lighthouse on the Shannon! Lord save us, how many times did I see it at night from the hill of Ballingarry! But there's no harbour, Matty.'

'There's the harbour at Foynes!'

'Oh, for God's sake!' she cried. 'That's miles and miles and miles away. 'Tis and twenty miles away! And where would you see any train, day or night, from anywhere at all near Ballyroche?'

They argued it hither and over until she suddenly found the coffee was gone cold and rushed away with the pot to the kitchen. Even there she kept up the argument, calling out that certainly, you could see Moneygay Castle, and the turn of the River Deel on a fine day, but no train, and then she went on about the steppingstones over the river, and came back babbling about Normoyle's bull that chased them across the dry river, one hot summer's day . . .

He said:

'Auntie! Why the hell did you never write home?'

'Not even once?' she said, with a crooked smile like a bold child.

'Not a sight nor a sound of you from the day you left Ballyroche, as my mother used to say, no more than if the earth swallowed you. You're a nice one!'

'Eat up!' she commanded him, with a little laugh and a tap on his wrist.

'Did you always live here, Auntie Lily?'

She sat down and put her face between her palms with her elbows on the table and looked at him.

'Here? Well, no . . . That is to say, no! My husband and me had a house of our very own over in East Fifty-eighth. He did very well for himself. He was quite a rich man when he died. A big jeweller. When he was killed in an airplane crash five years ago he left me very well off. But sure I didn't need a house of my own and I had lots of friends in Brooklyn, so I came to live here.'

67

'Fine! What more do you want, that is for a lone woman! No family?'

'I have my son. But he's married, to a Pole, they'll be over here first thing tomorrow morning to take me off to spend Christmas with them. They have an apartment on Riverside Drive. He is the manager of a big department store. Macy's on Flatbush Avenue. But tell me about Bid's children. You must have lots of brothers and sisters. Where are you going from here? Back to Ireland? To Limerick? To Ballyroche?'

He laughed.

'Where else would I go? Our next trip we hit the port of London. I'll be back like an arrow to Ballyroche. They'll be delighted to hear I met you. They'll be asking me all sorts of questions about you. Tell me more about your son, Auntie. Has he a family?'

'My son? Well, my son's name is Thomas. His wife's name is Catherine. She is very beautiful. She has means of her own. They are very happy. He is very well off. He's in charge of a big store Sears Roebuck on Bedford Avenue. Oh, a fine boy. Fine out! As you say. Fine out. He has three children. There's Cissy, and Matty. And . . .'

Her voice faltered. When she closed her eyes he saw how old she was. She rose and from the bottom dreawer of a chest of drawers she pulled out a photograph album. She laid it in front of him and sat back opposite him.

'That is my boy.'

When he said he was like her she said he was very like his father. Maxer said that he often heard that her husband was a most handsome man.

'Have you a picture of him?'

She drew the picture of her son towards her and looked down at it.

'Tell me more about Ballyroche,' she cried.

68

As he started into a long description of a harvest home he saw her eyes close again, and her breath came more heavily and he felt that she was not hearing a word he said. Then, suddenly, her palm slapped down on the picture of the young man, and he knew that she was not heeding him any more than if he wasn't there. Her fingers closed on the pasteboard. She shied it wildly across the room, where it struck the glass of the window flat on, hesitated and slid to the ground. Maxer saw snowflakes melting as often as they touched the pane. When he looked back at her she was leaning across the table, one white lock down over one eye, her yellow teeth bared.

'You spy!' she spat on him. 'You came from them! To spy on me!'

'I came from friendliness.'

'Or was it for a ha'porth of look-about? Well, you can go back to Ballyroche and tell 'em whatever you like. Tell 'em I'm starving if that'll please 'em, the mean, miserable, lousy set that never gave a damn about me from the day I left 'em. For forty years my own sister, your mother, never wrote one line to say . . .'

'You know damn well she'd have done anything for you if she only knew where you were. Her heart was stuck in you. The two of you were inside one another's pockets. My God, she was forever talking and talking about you. Morning, noon and night . . .'

She shouted at him across the table.

'I wrote six letters . . .'

'She never got them.'

'I registered two of them.'

'Nobody ever got a line from you, or about you, only for the one letter from the priest that married you to say you were well and happy.'

'What he wrote was that I was down and out. I saw

69

the letter. I let him send it. That Wop left me flat in this city with my baby. I wrote to everybody – my mother, my father, to Bid after she was your mother and had a home of her own. I had to work every day of my life. I worked today. I'll work tomorrow. If you want to know what I do I clean out offices. I worked to bring up my son, and what did he do? Walked out on me with that Polack of his and that was the last I saw of him, or her, or any human being belonging to me until I saw you. Tell them every word of it. They'll love it!'

Maxer got up and went over slowly to the bed for his jacket. As he buttoned it he looked at her glaring at him across the table. Then he looked away from her at the snowflakes feeling the windowpane and dying there. He said quitely:

'They're all dead. As for Limerick – I haven't been back to Ireland for eight years. When my mum died my father got married again. I ran away to sea when I was sixteen.'

He took his cap. When he was at the door he heard a chair fall and then she was at his side, holding his arm, whispering gently to him:

'Don't go away, Matty.' Her pallid eyes were flooded. 'For God's sake, don't leave me alone with *them* on Christmas Eve!'

Maxer stared at her. Her lips were wavering as if a wind were blowing over them. She had the face of a frightened girl. He threw his cap on the bed and went over and sat down beside it. While he sat there like a big baboon, with his hands between his knees, looking at the snowflakes, she raced into the kitchen to put on the kettle for rum punch. It was a long while before she brought in the two big glasses of punch, with orange sliced in them, and brown sugar like drowned sand at the base of them. When she held them out to him he looked first at them, and then at her, so timid, so pleading, and he began to laugh and laugh – a laugh that he choked by covering his eyes with his hands.

'Damn ye!' he groaned into his hands. 'I was better off drunk.'

She sat beside him on the bed. He looked up. He took one of the glasses and touched hers with it.

'Here's to poor Lily!' he smiled.

She fondled his free hand.

'Lovie, tell me this one thing and tell me true. Did she really and truly talk about me? Or was that all lies too?'

'She'd be crying rain down when she'd be talking about you. She was always and ever talking about you. She was mad about you.'

She sighed a long sigh.

'For years I couldn't understand it. But when my boy left me for that Polack I understood it. I guess Bid had a tough time bringing you all up. And there's no one more hard in all the world than a mother when she's thinking of her own. I'm glad she talked about me. It's better than nothing.'

They sat there on the bed talking and talking. She made more punch, and then more, and in the end they finished the bottle between them, talking about everybody either of them had known in or within miles of the County Limerick. They fixed to spend Christmas Day together, and have Christmas dinner downtown, and maybe go to a picture and then come back and talk some more.

Every time Maxer comes to New York he rings her number. He can hardly breathe until he hears her voice saying, 'Hello Matty.' They go on the town and have dinner, always at some place with an Irish name, or a green neon shamrock above the door, and then they go to a movie or a show, and then come back to

71

her room to have a drink and a talk about his last voyage, or the picture post cards he sent her, his latest bits and scraps of news about the Shannon shore. They always get first-class service in restaurants, although Maxer never noticed it until the night a waiter said, 'And what's mom having?' at which she gave him a slow wink out of her pale Limerick eyes and a slow, lover's smile.

THE TIME OF YEAR

WILLIAM TREVOR

All that autumn, when they were both fourteen, they had talked about their Christmas swim. She'd had the idea: that on Christmas morning when everyone was still asleep they would meet by the boats on the strand at Ballyquin and afterwards quite casually say that they had been for a swim on Christmas Day. Whenever they met during that stormy October and November they wondered how fine the day might be, how cold or wet, and if the sea could possibly be frozen. They walked together on the cliffs, looking down at the breaking waves of the Atlantic, shivering in anticipation. They walked through the misty dusk of the town, lingering over the first signs of Christmas in the shops; coloured lights strung up, holly and Christmas trees and tinsel. They wondered if people guessed about them. They didn't want them to, they wanted it to be a secret. People would laugh because they were children. They were in love that autumn.

Six years later Valerie still remembered, poignantly, in November. Dublin, so different from Ballyquin, stirred up the past as autumn drifted into winter and winds bustled around the grey buildings of Trinity College, where she was now a student. The city's trees were bleakly bare, it seemed to Valerie; there was sadness, even, on the lawns of her hall of residence, scattered with finished leaves. In her small room, preparing herself one Friday evening for the Skullys' end-of-term party, she sensed quite easily the Christ-was chill of the sea, the chilliness creeping slowly over her calves and knees. She paused with the memory, gazing at herself in the looking-glass attached to the inside of her cupboard door. She was a tall girl, standing now in a white silk petticoat, with a thin face and thin long fingers and an almost classical nose. Her black hair was as straight as a die, falling to her shoulders. She was pretty when she smiled and she did so at her reflection, endeavouring to overcome the melancholy that visited her at this time of year. She turned away and picked up a green corduroy dress which she had laid out on her bed. She was going to be late if she dawdled like this.

The parties given by Professor and Mrs Skully were renowned neither for the entertainment they provided nor for their elegance. They were, unfortunately, difficult to avoid, the Professor being persistent in the face of repeated excuseds – a persistence it was deemed unwise to strain.

Bidden for half past seven, his History students came on bicycles, a few in Kilroy's Mini, Ruth Cusper on her motorcycle, Bewley Joal on foot. Woodward, Whipp and Woolmer-Mills came cheerfully, being kindred spirits of the Professor's and in no way dismayed by the immediate prospect. Others were apprehensive or cross, trying not to let it show as smilingly they entered the Skullys' house in Rathgar.

'How very nice!' Mrs Skully murmured in a familiar manner in the hall. 'How jolly good of you to come.'

The hall was not yet decorated for Christmas, but the Professor had found the remains of last year's crackers and had stuck half a dozen behind the heavily framed scenes of Hanover that had been established in the hall since the early days of the Skully's marriage. The gaudy crêpe paper protruded

74

above the pictures in splurges of green, red and yellow, and cheered up the hall to a small extent. The coloured scarves and overcoats of the History students, already accumulating on the hall-stand, did so more effectively.

In the Skullys' sitting-room the Professor's record-player, old and in some way special, was in its usual place: on a mahogany table in front of the French windows, which were now obscured by brown curtains. Four identical rugs, their colour approximately matching that of the curtains, were precisely arranged on darker brown linoleum. Rexine-seated dining-chairs lined brownish walls.

The Professor's History students lent temporary character to this room, as their coats and scarves did to the hall. Kilroy was plump in a royal-blue suit. The O'Neill sisters' cluster of followers, jostling even now for promises of favours, wore carefully pressed denim or tweed. The O'Neill sisters themselves exuded a raffish, cocktail-time air. They were twins, from Lurgan, both of them blonde and both favouring an excess of eye-shadow, with lipstick that wetly gleamed, the same shade of pink as the trouser suits that nudgingly hugged the protuberances of their bodies. Not far from where they now held court, the rimless spectacles of Bewley Joal had a busy look in the room's harsh light; the complexion of Yvonne Smith was displayed to disadvantage. So was the troublesome fair hair of Honor Hitchcock, who was engaged to a student known as the Reverend because of his declared intention one day to claim the title. Cosily in a corner she linked her arm with his, both of them seeming middle-aged before their time, inmates already of a draughty rectory in Co. Cork or Clare. 'I'll be the first,' Ruth Cusper vowed, 'to visit you in your parish. Wherever it is.' Ruth Cusper was a statuesque

English girl, not yet divested of her motor-cycling gear.

The colours worn by the girls, and the denim and tweed, and the royal blue of Kilroy, contrasted sharply with the uncared-for garb of Woodward, Whipp and Woolmer-Mills, all of whom were expected to take Firsts. Stained and frayed, these three hung together without speaking, Woodward very tall, giving the impression of an etiolated newt, Whipp small, his glasses repaired with Sellotape, Woolmer-Mills for ever launching himself back and forth on the balls of his feet.

In a pocket of Kilroy's suit there was a miniature bottle of vodka, for only tea and what the Professor described as 'cup' were served in the course of the evening. Kilroy fingered it, smiling across the room at the Professor, endeavouring to give the impression that he was delighted to be present. He was a student who was fearful of academic failure, his terror being that he would not get a Third: he had set his sights on a Third, well aware that to have set them higher would not be wise. He brought his little bottles of vodka to the Professor's parties as an act of bravado, a gesture designed to display jauntiness, to show that he could take a chance. But the chances he took with his vodka were not great.

Bewley Joal, who would end up with a respectable Second, was laying down the law to Yvonne Smith, who would be grateful to end up with anything at all. Her natural urge to chatter was stifled, for no one could get a word in when the clanking voice of Bewley Joal was in full flow. 'Oh, it's far more than just a solution, dear girl,' he breezily pronounced, speaking of Moral Rearmament. Yvonne Smith nodded and agreed, trying to say that an aunt of hers thought most highly of Moral Rearmament, that she herself had always been meaning to look into it. But the voice of Bewley Joal cut all her sentences in half.

'I thought we'd start,' the Professor anounced, having coughed and cleared his throat, 'with the *Pathétique*.' He fiddled with the record-player while everyone sat down, Ruth Cusper on the floor. He was a biggish man in a grey suit that faintly recalled the clothes of Woodward, Whipp and Woolmer-Mills. On a large head hair was still in plentiful supply even though the Professor was fifty-eight. The hair was grey also, bushing out around his head in a manner that suggested professorial vagueness rather than a gesture in the direction of current fashion. His wife, who stood by his side while he placed a record on the turntable, wore a magenta skirt and twin-set, and a string of jade beads. In almost every way – including this lively choice of dress – she seemed naturally to complement her husband, to fill the gaps his personality couldn't be bothered with. Her nervous manner was the opposite of his confident one. He gave his parties out of duty, and having done so found it hard to take an interest in any students except those who had already proved themselves academically sound. Mrs Skully preferred to strike a lighter note. Now and again she made efforts to entice a few of the girls to join her on Saturday evenings, offering the suggestion that they might listen together to Saturday Night Theatre and afterwards sit around and discuss it. Because the Professor saw no point in television there was none in the Skullys' house.

Tchaikovsky filled the sitting-room. The Professor sat down and then Mrs Skully did. The doorbell rang.

'Ah, of course,' Mrs Skully said.

'Valerie Upcott,' Valerie said. 'Good evening, Mrs Skully.'

'Come in, come in, dear. The *Patrhétique*'s just started.' She remarked in the hall on the green corduroy dress that was revealed when Valerie took off her coat. The green was of so dark a shade that it might almost have been black. It had large green buttons all down the front. 'Oh, how really nice!' Mrs Skully said.

The crackers that decorated the scenes of Hanover looked sinister, Valerie thought: Christmas was on the way, soon there'd be the coloured lights and imitation snow. She smiled at Mrs Skully. She wondered about saying that her magenta outfit was nice also, but decided against it. 'We'll slip in quietly,' Mrs Skully said.

Valerie tried to forget the crackers as she entered the sitting-room and took her place on a chair, but in her mind the brash images remained. They did so while she acknowledged Kilroy's winking smile and while she glanced towards the Professor in case he chose to greet her. But the Professor, his head bent over clasped hands, did not look up.

Among the History students Valerie was an unknown quantity. During the two years they'd all known one another she'd established herself as a person who was particularly quiet. She had a private look even when she smiled and the thin features of her face were startled out of tranquillity, as if an electric light had suddenly been turned on. Kilroy still tried to take her out, Ruth Cusper was pally. But Valerie's privacy, softened by her sudden smile, unfussily repelled these attentions.

For her part she was aware of the students' curiosity, and yet she could not have said to any one of them that a tragedy which had occurred was not properly in the past yet. She could not mention the tragedy to people who didn't know about it already. She couldn't tell it as a story because to her it didn't seem in the least like that. It was a fact you had to live with, half wanting to forget it, half feeling you could not. This time of year and the first faint signs of Christmas were enough to tease it brightly into life.

The second movement of the *Pathétique* came to an end, the Professor rose to turn the record over, the students murmured. Mrs Skully slipped away, as she always did at this point, to attend to matters in the kitchen. While the Professor was bent over the record-player Kilroy waved his bottle of vodka about and then raised it to his lips. 'Hullo, Valerie,' Yvonne Smith whispered across the distance that separated them. She endeavoured to continue her communication by shaping words with her lips. Valerie smiled at her and at Ruth Cusper, who had turned her head when she'd heard Yvonne Smith's greeting. 'Hi,' Ruth Cusper said.

The music began again. The mouthing of Yvonne Smith continued for a moment and then ceased. Valerie didn't notice that, because in the room the students and the Professor were shadows of a kind, the music a distant piping. The swish of wind was in the room, and the shingle, cold on her bare feet; so were the two flat stones they'd placed on their clothes to keep them from blowing away. White flecks in the air were snow, she said: Christmas snow, what everyone wanted. But he said the flecks were flecks of foam.

He took her hand, dragging her a bit because the shingle hurt the soles of her feet and slowed her down. He hurried on the sand, calling back to her, reminding her that it was her idea, laughing at her hesitation. He called out something else as he ran into the breakers, but she couldn't hear because of the roar of the sea. She stood in the icy shallows and when she heard him

79

shouting again she imagined he was still mocking her. She didn't even know he was struggling, she wasn't in the least aware of his death. It was his not being there she noticed, the feeling of being alone on the strand at Ballyquin.

'Cup, Miss Upcott?' the Professor offered in the dining-room. Poised above a glass, a jug contained a yellowish liquid. She said she'd rather have tea.

There were egg sandwiches and cakes, plates of crisps, biscuits and Twiglets. Mrs Skully poured tea, Ruth Cusper handed round the cups and saucers. The O'Neill sisters and their followers shared an obscene joke, which was a game that had grown up at the Skullys' parties: one student doing his best to make the others giggle too noisily. A point was gained if the Professor demanded to share the fun.

'Oh, but of course there isn't any argument,' Bewley Joal was insisting, still talking to Yvonne Smith about Moral Rearmament. Words had ceased to dribble from her lips. Instead she kept nodding her head. 'We live in times of decadence,' Bewley Joal pronounced.

Woodward, Whipp and Woolmer-Mills were still together, Woolmer-Mills launching himself endlessly on to the balls of his feet, Whipp sucking at his cheeks. No conversation was taking place among them: when the Professor finished going round with his jug of cup, talk of some kind would begin, probably about a mediæval document Woodward had earlier mentioned. Or about a reference to *panni streit sine grano* which had puzzled Woolmer-Mills.

'Soon be Christmas,' Honor Hitchcock remarked to Valerie.

'Yes, it will.'

'I love it. I love the way you can imagine everyone doing just the same things on Christmas Eve, tying up presents, running around with holly, listening to the carols. And Christmas Day: that same meal in millions of houses, and the same prayers. All over the world.

'Yes, there's that.'

'Oh, I think it's marvellous.'

'Christmas?' Kilroy said, suddenly beside them. He laughed, the fat on his face shaking a bit. 'Much overrated in my small view.' He glanced as he spoke at the Professor's profile, preparing himself in case the Professor should look in his direction. His expression changed, becoming solemn.

There were specks of dandruff, Valerie noticed, on the shoulders of the Professor's grey suit. She thought it odd that Mrs Skully hadn't drawn his attention to them. She thought it odd that Kilroy was so determined about his Third. And that Yvonne Smith didn't just walk away from the clanking voice of Bewley Joal.

'Orange or coffee?' Ruth Cusper proffered two cakes that had been cut into slices. The fillings in Mrs Skully's cakes were famous, made with Trex and caster sugar. The cakes themselves had a flat appearance, like large biscuits.

'I wouldn't touch any of that stuff,' Kilroy advised, jocular again. 'I was up all night after it last year.'

'Oh, nonsense!' Ruth Cusper placed a slice of orange cake on Valerie's plate, making a noise that indicated she found Kilroy's attempt at wit a failure. She passed on, and Kilroy without reason began to laugh.

Valerie looked at them, her eyes pausing on each face in the room. She was different from these people of her own age because of her autumn melancholy and the bitterness of Christmas. A solitude had been made for her, while they belonged to each other, separate yet part of a whole.

She thought about them, envying them their

ordinary normality, the good fortune they accepted as their due. They trailed no horror, no ghosts or images that wouldn't go away: you could tell that by looking at them. Had she herself already been made peculiar by all of it, eccentric and strange and edgy? And would it never slip away, into the past where it belonged? Each year it was the same, no different from the year before, intent on hanging on to her. Each year she smiled and made an effort. She was brisk with it, she did her best. She told herself she had to live with it, agreeing with herself that of course she had to, as if wishing to be overheard. And yet to die so young, so pointlessly and so casually, seemed to be something you had to feel unhappy about. It dragged out tears from you; it made you hesitate again, standing in the icy water. Your idea it had been.

'Tea, you people?' Mrs Skully offered.

'Awfully kind of you, Mrs Skully,' Kilroy said. 'Splendid tea this is.'

'I should have thought you'd be keener on the Professor's cup, Mr Kilroy.'

'No, I'm not a cup man, Mrs Skully.'

Valerie wondered what it would be like to be Kilroy. She wondered about his private thoughts, even what he was thinking now as he said he wasn't a cup man. She imagined him in his bedroom, removing his royal-blue suit and meticulously placing it on a hanger, talking to himself about the party, wondering if he had done himself any damage in the Professor's eyes. She imagined him as a child, plump in bathing-trunks, building a sandcastle. She saw him in a kitchen, standing on a chair by an open cupboard, nibbling the corner of a Chivers' jelly.

She saw Ruth Cusper too, bossy at a children's party, friendly bossy, towering over other children. She made them play a game and wasn't disappointed

82

when they didn't like it. You couldn't hurt Ruth Cusper; she'd grown an extra skin beneath her motor-cycling gear. At night, she often said, she fell asleep as soon as her head touched the pillow.

You couldn't hurt Bewley Joal, either: a grasping child Valerie saw him as, watchful and charmless. Once he'd been hurt, she speculated: another child had told him that no one enjoyed playing with him, and he'd resolved from that moment not to care about stuff like that, to push his way through other people's opinion of him, not wishing to know it.

As children, the O'Neill sisters teased; their faithful tormentors pulled their hair. Woodward, Whipp and Woolmer-Mills read the *Children's Encyclopaedia*. Honor Hitchcock and the Reverend played mummies and daddies. 'Oh, listen to that chatterbox!' Yvonne Smith's father dotingly cried, affection that Yvonne Smith had missed ever since.

In the room the clanking of Bewley Joal punctuated the giggling in the corner where the O'Neill sisters were. More tea was poured and more of the Professor's cup, more cake was handed round. 'Ah, yes,' the Professor began. *'Panni streit sine grano.'* Woodward, Whipp and Woolmer-Mills bent their heads to listen.

The Professor, while waiting on his upstairs landing for Woolmer-Mills to use the lavatory, spoke of the tomatoes he grew. Similarly delayed downstairs, Mrs Skully suggested to the O'Neill sisters that they might like, one Saturday night next term, to listen to Saturday Night Theatre with her. It was something she enjoyed, she said, especially the discussion after-wards. 'Or you, Miss Upcott,' she said. 'You've never been to one of my evenings either.'

Valerie smiled politely, moving with Mrs Skully towards the sitting-room, where Tchaikovsky once

more resounded powerfully. Again she examined the
arrayed faces. Some eyes were closed in sleep, others
were weary beneath a weight of tedium. Woodward's
newt-like countenance had not altered, nor had
Kilroy's fear dissipated. Frustration still tugged at
Yvonne Smith. Nothing much was happening in the
face of Mrs Skully.

Valerie continued to regard Mrs Skully's face and
suddenly she found herself shivering. How could that
mouth open and close, issuing invitations without
knowing they were the subject of derision? How
could this woman, in her late middle age, officiate at
student parties in magenta and jade, or bake inedible
cakes without knowing it? How could she daily
permit herself to be taken for granted by a man who
cared only for students with academic success behind
them? How could she have married his pomposity in
the first place? There was something wrong with Mrs
Skully, there was something missing, as if some part
of her had never come to life. The more Valerie
examined her the more extraordinary Mrs Skully
seemed, and then it seemed extraordinary that the
Professor should be unaware that no one lilked his
parties. It was as if some part of him hadn't come to
life either, as if they lived together in the dead wood of
a relationship, together in this house because it was
convenient.

She wondered if the other students had ever
thought that, or if they'd be bothered to survey in any
way whatsoever the Professor and his wife. She
wondered if they saw a reflection of the Skullys'
marriage in the brownness of the room they all sat in,
or in the crunchy fillings of Mrs Skullly's cakes, or in
the Rexine-seated dining-chairs that were not
comfortable. You couldn't blame them for not
wanting to think about the Skullys' marriage: what

good could come of it? The other students were busy and more organised than she. They had aims in life. They had failures she could sense, as she had sensed their pasts. Honor Hitchcock and the Reverend would settle down as right as rain in a provincial rectory, the followers of the O'Neill sisters would enter various business worlds. Woodward, Whipp and Woolmer-Mills would be the same as the Professor, dandruff on the shoulders of three grey suits. Bewley Joal would rise to heights, Kilroy would not. Ruth Cusper would run a hall of residence, the O'Neill sisters would give two husbands hell in Lurgan. Yvonne Smith would live in hopes.

The music of Tchaikovsky gushed over these reflections, as if to soften some harshness in them. But to Valerie there was no harshness in her contemplation of these people's lives, only fact and a lacing of speculation. The Skullys would go on ageing and he might never turn to his wife and say he was sorry. The O'Neill sisters would lose their beauty and Bewley Joal his vigour. One day Woolmer-Mills would find that he could no longer launch himself on to the balls of his feet. Kilroy would enter a home for the senile. Death would shatter the cotton-wool cosiness of Honor Hitchcock and the Reverend.

She wondered what would happen if she revealed what she had thought, if she told them that in order to keep her melancholy in control she had played about with their lives, seeing them in childhood, visiting them with old age and death. Which of them would seek to stop her while she cited the arrogance of the Professor and the pusillanimity of his wife? She heard her own voice echoing in a silence, telling them finally, in explanation, of the tragedy in her own life.

'Please all have a jolly Christmas,' Mrs Skully urged in

the hall as scarves and coats were lifted from the hall-stand. 'Please now.'

'We shall endeavour,' Kilroy promised, and the others made similar remarks, wishing Mrs Skully a happy Christmas herself, thanking her and the Professor for the party. Kilroy adding that it had been most enjoyable. There'd be another, the Professor promised, in May.

There was the roar of Ruth Cusper's motor-cycle, and the overloading of Kilroy's Mini, and the striding into the night of Bewley Joal, and others making off on bicycles. Valerie walked with Yvonne Smith through the suburban roads. 'I quite like Joal,' Yvonne Smith confided, releasing the first burst of her pent-up chatter. 'He's all right, isn't he? Quite nice, really, quite clever. I mean, if you care for a clever kind of person. I mean, I wouldn't mind going out with him if he asked me.'

Valerie agreed that Bewley Joal was all right if you cared for that kind of person. It was pleasant in the cold night air. It was good that the party was over.

Yvonne Smith said good-night, still chattering about Bewley Joal as she turned into the house where her lodgings were. Valerie walkled on alone, a thin shadow in the gloom. Compulsively now, she thought about the party, seeing again the face of Mrs Skully and the Professor's face and the faces of the others. They formed, like a backdrop in her mind, an assembly as vivid as the tragedy that more grimly visited it. They seemed like the other side of the tragedy, as if she had for the first time managed to peer round a corner. The feeling puzzled her. It was odd to be left with it after the Skullys' end-of-term party.

In the garden of the hall of residence the fallen leaves were sodden beneath her feet as she crossed a lawn to shorten her journey. The bewilderment she felt lifted a little. She had been wrong to imagine she envied other people their normality and good fortune. She was as she wished to be. She paused in faint moonlight, repeating that to herself and then repeating it again. She did not quite add that the tragedy had made her what she was, that without it she would not possess her reflective introspection, or be sensitive to more than just the time of year. But the thought hovered with her as she moved towards the lights of the house, offering what appeared to be a hint of comfort.

FATHER CHRISTMAS

MICHAEL McLAVERTY

'Will you do what I ask you?" his wife said again, wiping the crumbs off the newspaper which served as a tablecloth. 'Wear your hard hat and you'll get the job.'

He didn't answer her or raise his head. He was seated on the dilapidated sofa lacing his boots, and behind him tumbled two of his children, each chewing a crust of bread. His wife paused, a hand on her hip. She glanced at the sleety rain falling into the backyard, turned round, and threw the crumbs into the fire.

'You'll wear it, John – won't you?'

Again he didn't answer though his mind was already made up. He strode into the scullery and while he washed himself she took an overcoat from a nail behind the kitchen door, brushed it vigorously, gouging out the specks of dirt with the nose of the brush. She put it over the back of a chair and went upstairs for his hard hat.

'I'm a holy show in that article,' he said, when she was handing him the hat and helping him into the overcoat. 'I'll be a nice ornament among the other applicants! I wish you'd leave me alone!'

'You look respectable anyhow. I could take a fancy for you all over again,' and she kissed him playfully on the side of the cheek.

'If I don't get the job you needn't blame me. I've done all you asked – every mortal thing.'

'You'll get it all right – never you fear. I know what

I'm talking about.'

He hurried out of the street in case some of the neighbours would ask him if he were going to a funeral, and when he had taken his place in the line of young men who were all applying for the job of Father Christmas in the Big Store he was still conscious of the bowler hat perched on top of his head. He was a timid little man and he tried to crouch closer to the wall and make himself inconspicuous amongst the group of grey-capped men. The rain continued to fall as they waited for the door to open and he watched the drops clinging to the peaks of their caps, swelling and falling to the ground.

'If he had a beard we could all go home,' he heard someone say, and he felt his ears reddening, aware that the remark was cast at him. But later when he was following the Manager up the brass-lipped stairs, after he had got the job, he dwelt on the wisdom of his wife and knew that the hat had endowed him with an air of shabby respectability.

'Are you married?' the Manager had asked him, looking at the nervous way he turned the hat in his hand. 'And have you any children?' He had answered everything with a meek smile and the Manager told him to stand aside until he had interviewed, as a matter of form, the rest of the applicants.

And then the interviews were quickly over, and when the Manager and John were mounting the stairs he saw a piece of caramel paper sticking to the Manager's heel. Down a long aisle they passed with rows of counters at each side and shoppers gathered round them. And though it was daylight outside, the electric lights were lit, and through the glare there arose a buzz of talk, the rattle of money, and the warm smell of new clothes and perfume and confectionery – all of it entering John's mind in a confused and dreamy fashion for his eye was fastened on the caramel paper as he followed respectfully after the Manager. Presently they emerged on a short flight of stairs where a notice – PRIVATE – on trestles straddled across it. The Manager lifted it ostentatiously to the side, ushered John forward with a sweep of his arm, and replaced the notice with mechanical importance.

'Just a minute,' said John, and he plucked the caramel paper from the Manager's heel, crumpled it between his fingers, and put it in his pocket.

They entered the quiet seclusion of a small room that had a choking smell of dust and cardboard boxes. The Manager mounted a step-ladder, and taking a large box from the top shelf looked at something written on the side, slapped the dust off it against his knee, and broke the string.

'Here,' he said, throwing down the box. 'You'll get a red cloak in that and a white beard.' He sat on the top rung of the ladder and held a false face on the tip of his finger: 'Somehow I don't think you'll need this. You'll do as you are. Just put on the beard and whiskers.'

'Whatever you say,' smiled John, for he always tried to please people.

Another box fell at his feet: 'You'll get a pair of top boots in that!' The Manager folded the step-ladder, and daintily picking pieces of fluff from his sleeves he outlined John's duties for the day and emphasised that after closing-time he'd have to make up parcels for the following day's sale.

Left alone John breathed freely, took off his overcoat and hung it at the back of the door, and for some reason whenever he crossed the floor he did so on his tiptoes. He lifted the red cloak that was trimmed with fur, held it in his outstretched arms to admire it, and squeezed the life out of a moth that was struggling in one of the folds. Chips of tinsel glinted on the shoulders of the cloak and he was ready to flick them off when he decided it was more Christmassy-looking to let them remain on. He pulled on the cloak, crossed on tiptoes to a looking-glass on the wall and winked and grimaced at himself, sometimes putting up the collar of the cloak to enjoy the warm touch of the fur on the back of his neck. He attached the beard and the whiskers, spitting out one or two hairs that had strayed into his mouth.

'The very I-T,' he said, and caught the beard in his fist and waggled it at his reflection in the mirror. 'Hello, Santa!' he smiled, and thought of his children and how they would laugh to see him togged up in this regalia. 'I must tell her to bring them down some day,' and he gave a twirl on his toes, making a heap of paper rustle in the corner.

He took off his boots, looked reflectively at the broken sole of each and pressed his thumb into the wet leather: 'Pasteboard – nothing else!' he said in disgust, and threw them on the heap of brown paper. He reached for the top boots that were trimmed with fur. They looked a bit on the small side. With some difficulty he squeezed his feet into them. He walked across the floor, examining the boots at each step; they were very tight for him, but he wasn't one to complain, and, after all, the job was only for the Christmas season and they'd be sure to stretch with the wearing.

When he was fully dressed he made his way down the stairs, lifted his leg over the trestle with the name PRIVATE and presented himself on one of the busy floors. A shop-girl, hesitating before striking the cash-register, smiled over at him. His face burned. Then a little girl plucked her mother's skirt and called, 'Oh, Mammy, there's Daddy Christmas!' With his hands in his wide sleeves he stood in a state of nervous perplexity till the shop-girl, scratching her head with the tip of her pencil, shouted jauntily: 'First Floor, Santa Claus, right on down the stairs!' He stumbled on the stairs because of the tight boots and when he halted to regain his composure he felt the bloody hammering in his temples and he wished now that he hadn't listened to his wife and worn his hard hat. She was always nagging at him, night, noon and morning, and he doing his damned best!

On the first floor the Manager beckoned him to a miniature house – a house painted in imitation brick, snow on the eaves, a door which he could enter by stooping low, and a chimney large enough to contain his head and shoulders, and inside the house stacks of boxes neatly piled, some in blue paper and others in pink.

The Manager produced a hand-bell. 'You stand here,' said the Manager, placing himself at the door of the house. 'Ring your bell a few times – like this. Then shout in a loud, commanding voice: "Roll up now! Blue for the Boys, and Pink for the Girls".' And he explained that when business was slack, he was to mount the ladder, descend the chimney, and bring up the parcels in that manner, but if there was a crowd he was just to open the door and shake hands with each child before presenting the boxes. They were all the same price – a shilling each.

For the first ten minutes or so John's voice was weak and self-conscious and the Manager, standing a short distance away, ordered him to raise his voice a little louder: 'You must attract attention – that's what you're paid for. Try it once again.'

'Blue for the Boys, and Pink for the Girls!' shouted John, and he imagined all the buyers at the neighbouring counters had paused to listen to him. 'Blue for the Boys, and Pink for the Girls!' he repeated, his eye on the Manager who was judging him from a distance. The Manager smiled his approval and then shook an imaginary bell in the air. John suddenly remembered about the bell in his hand and he shook it vigorously, but a shop-girl tightened up her face at him and he folded his fingers over the skirt of the bell in order to muffle the sound. He gained more confidence, but as his nervousness decreased he became aware of the tight boots imprisoning his feet, and occasionally he would disappear into his little house and catching the sole of each in turn he would stretch them across his knee.

But the children gave him no peace, and with his head held genially to the side, if the Manager were watchig him, he would smile broadly and listen with affected interest to each child's demand.

'Please, Santa Claus, bring me a tricycle at Christmas and a doll's pram for Angela.'

'I'll do that! Everything you want,' said Father Christmas expansively, and he patted the little boy on the head with gentle dignity before handing him a blue parcel. But when he raised his eyes to the boy's mother she froze him with a look.

'I didn't think you would have any tricycles this year,' she said. 'I thought you were only making wooden trains.'

'Oh, yes! No, yes. Not at all! Yes, of course, I'll get you a nice wooden train,' Father Christmas turned to the boy in confusion. 'If you keep good I'll have a lovely train for you.'

'I don't want an oul' train. I want a tricycle,' the boy whimpered, clutching his blue-papered parcel.

'I couldn't make any tricycles this year,' consoled Father Christmas. 'My reindeer were sick and three of them died on me.'

The boy's mother smiled and took him by the hand.

'Now, pet, didn't I tell you Santa had no tricycles? You better shout up the chimney for something else - a nice game or a wooden train.'

'I don't want an oul' game – I want a tricycle,' he cried, and jigged his feet.

'You'll get a warm ear if you're not careful. Come on now and none of your nonsense. And Daddy Christmas after giving you a nice box, all for yourself.'

Forcibly she led the boy away and John, standing with his hands in his sleeves, felt the prickles of sweat on his forehead and resolved to promise nothing to the children until he had got the cue from the parents.

As the day progressed he climbed up the ladder and down the chimney, emerging again with his arms laden with parcels. His feet tortured him and when he glanced at the boots every wrinkle in the leather was smoothed away. He couldn't continue like this all day; it would drive him mad.

'Roll up!' he bawled. 'Roll up! Blue for the Pinks and Boys for the Girls! Roll up, I say. Blue for the Pinks and Boys for the Girls.' Then he stopped and repeated the same mistake before catching himself up. And once more he clanged the bell with subdued ferocity till its sound drowned the jingle of the cash-registers and the shop-girls had to shout to be heard.

At one o'clock he wearily climbed the stairs to the quiet room, where dinner was brought to him on a tray. He took off his boots and gazed sympathetically at his crushed toes. He massaged them tenderly, and when he had finished his dinner he pared his corns with a razor blade he had bought at one of the counters. He now squeezed his bare feet into the boots, walked across the room, and sat down again, his face twisted with despair. 'Why do I always give in to that woman,' he said aloud to himself. 'I've no strength – no power to stand up and shout in her face:

"No, no, no! I'll go my own way in my own time!"' He'd let her know tonight the agony he suffered, and his poor feet gathered up all day like a rheumatic fist.

Calmed after this outburst, and reassuring himself that the job was only for three weeks, he gave a 2whistle of forced satisfaction, brushed the corn-parings off the chair, and went off to stand outside the little house with its imitation snow on the chimney.

The afternoon was the busiest time, and he was glad to be able to stand at the door like a human being and hand out the parcels, instead of ascending and descending the ladder like a trained monkey. When the children crowded too close to him he kept them at arm's length in case they'd trample on his feet. But he always managed to smile as he watched them shaking their boxes or tearing holes in the paper in an effort to guess what was inside. And the parents smiled too when they looked at him wagging his finger at the little girls and promising them dolls at Christmas if they would go to bed early, eat their porridge and stop biting their nails. But before closing time a woman was back holding an untidy parcel. 'That's supposed to be for a boy,' she said peevishly.

'There's a rubber doll in it and my wee boy has cried his eyes out ever since.'

'I'm just new to the job,' Father Christmas apologised. 'It'll never occur again.' And he tossed the parcel into the house and handed the woman a new one.

At the end of his day he had gathered from the floor a glove with a hole in one finger, three handkerchiefs, a necklace of blue beads, and a child's handbag containing a halfpenny and three tram-tickets. When he was handing them to the Manager he wondered if he should complain about the boots, but the tired look on the Manager's face and his reminder about staying

95

behind to make up parcels discouraged him.

For the last time he climbed the stairs, took off his boots and flung them from him, and as he prepared the boxes he padded about the cool floor in his bare feet, and to ensure that he wouldn't make a mistake he arranged, at one side of the room, the contents for the girls' boxes: dolls, shops, pages of transfers, story books, and crayons; and at the opposite side of the room the toys for the boys: ludo, snakes and ladders, blow football, soldiers, cowboy outfits, and wooden whistles. And as he parcelled them neatly and made loops in the twine for the children's fingers he decided once again to tell his wife to bring his own kids along and he'd have special parcels prepared for them.

On his way out of the Store the floors were silent and deserted, the counters humped with cavnas covers, and the little house looking strangely real now under a solitary light. A mouse nibbling at something on the floor sucrried off between an alleyway in the counters, and on the ground floor two women were sweeping up the dust and gossiping loudly.

The caretaker let him out by a side door, and as he walked off in the rain through the lamp-lighted streets he put up the collar of his coat and avoided the puddles as best he could. A sullen resentment seized his heart and he began to drag from the corners of his mind the things that irritated him. He thought they should have given him tea before he left, or even a bun and a glass of milk, and he thought of his home and maybe the fine tea his wife would have for him, and a good fire in the grate and the kids in bed. He walked more quickly. He passed boys eating chip potatoes out of a newspaper, and he stole a glance at Joe Raffo's chip-shop and the cloud of steam rolling through the open door into the cold air. The smell maddened him.

He plunged his hands into his pockets and fiddled with a button, bits of hard crumbs, and a sticky bit of caramel paper. He took out the caramel paper and threw it on the wet street.

He felt cheated and discontented with everything; and the more he thought of the job the more he blamed his wife for all the agony he had suffered throughout the day. She couldn't leave him alone – not for one solitary minute could she let him have a thought of his own or come to a decision of his own. She must be for ever interfering, barging in, and poking into his business. He was a damned fool to listen to her and to don a ridiculous hard hat for such a miserable job. Father Christmas and his everlasting smile! He'd smile less if he had to wear a pair of boots three sizes too small for him. It was a young fella they wanted for the job – somebody accustomed to standing for hours at a street corner and measuring the legth of his spits on the kerb. And then the ladder! That was the bloody limit! Up and down, down and up, like a squirrel in a cage, instead of giving you a stick and a chair where you could sit and really look like an old man. When he'd get home he'd let his wife know what she let him in for. It would lead to a row between them, and when that happened she'd go about for days flinging his meals on the table and belting the kids for sweet damn-all. He'd have to tell her – it was no use suffering devil's torture and saying nothing about it. But then, it's more likely than not she'd put on her hat and coat and go down to the Manager in the morning and complain about the boots, and then he might lose the job, bad and all as it was. Och, he'd say nothing – sure, bad temper never got you anywhere!

He stepped into a puddle to avoid a man's umbrella and when he felt the cold splash of water up the leg of his trousers his anger surged back again. He'd tell her all. He'd soon take the wind out of her sails and her self-praise about the hat! He'd tell her everything.

He hurried up the street and at the door of his house he let down the collar of his coat and shook the rain off his hat. He listened for a minute and heard the children shouting. He knocked, and the three of them pounded to the door to open it.

'It's Daddy,' they shouted, but he brushed past them without speaking.

His wife was washing the floor in the kitchen and as she wrung the cloth into the bucket and brushed back her hair with the back of her hand she looked at him with a bright smile.

'You got it all right?'

'Why aren't the children in bed?'

'I didn't expect you home so soon.'

'Did you think I was a bus conductor!'

She noticed the hard ring in his voice. She rubbed the soap on the scrubber and hurried to finish her work, making great whorls and sweeps with the cloth. She took off her dirty apron, and as she washed and dried her hands in the scullery she glanced in at him seated on the sofa, his head resting on his hands, the three children waiting for him to speak to them. 'It was the hat,' she said to herself. 'It was the hat that did the trick.'

'Come on now and up to bed quickly,' and she clapped her hands at the children.

'But you have to wash our legs in the bucket.'

'You'll do all right for tonight. Your poor father's hungry after his hard day's work.' And as she pulled off a jersey she held it in her hand and gave the fire a poke under the kettle. John stared into the fire and when he raised his foot there was a damp imprint left on the tiles. She handed him a pair of warm socks from the line and a pair of old slippers that she had made for him out of pasteboard and a piece of velours.

'I've a nice bit of steak for your tea,' she said. 'I'll put on the pan when I get these ones into their beds.'

He rubbed his feet and pulled on the warm socks. It was good that she hadn't the steak fried and lying as dry as a stick in the oven. When all was said and done, she had some sense in her head.

The children began to shout up the chimney telling Santa Claus what they wanted for Christmas, and when they knelt to say their prayers they had to thank God for sending their Daddy a good job. John smiled for the first time since he came into the house and he took the youngest on his knee. 'You'll get a doll and a pram for Christmas,' he said, 'and Johnny will get a wooden train with real wheels and Pat – what will we get him?' And he remembered putting a cowboy's outfit into one of the boxes. 'A cowboy's outfit – hat and gun.'

His wife had put the pan on the fire and already the steak was frizzling. 'Don't let that pan burn till I come down again. I'll not be a minute.'

He heard her put the kids to bed, and in a few minutes she was down again, a fresh blouse on her and a clean apron.

She poured out his tea and after he had taken a few mouthfuls he began to tell her about the crowd of applicants and about the fellow who shouted: 'We'd better all go home,' when he had seen him in the hat.

'He was jealous – that's what was wrong with him!' she said. 'A good clout on the ear he needed.'

He told her about the Manager, the handbell, the blue and pink parcels, the little house, and the red cloak he had to wear. Then he paused, took a drink of tea, cut a piece of bread into three bits, and went on eating slowly.

'It's well you took my advice and wore the hat,' she said brightly. 'I knew what I was talking about. And you look so – so manly in it.' She remembered about the damp stain on the floor, and she lifted his boots off the fender and looked at the broken soles. 'They're done,' she said, 'that's the first call in your wages at the end of the week.'

He got up from the table and sat near the fire. She handed him his pipe filled with tobacco, and as she washed the dishes in the scullery she would listen to the little pouts he made while he smoked. Now and again she glanced in at him, at the contented look on his face and the steam arising from his boots on the fender.

She took off her apron, tidied her hair at the looking-glass, and powdered her face. She stole across the floor to him as he sat staring into the fire. Quietly she took the pipe from his lips and put it on the mantelpiece. She smiled at him and he smiled back, and as she stooped to kiss him he knew that he would say nothing to her now about the tight boots.

APACHES

PAT McCABE

The snow came and then the apaches, sitting there in the hollow, a thin snake of purple smoke unwinding from a fire of blackened stones, the old squaw sucking a small pipe through teeth the colour of wood. A prairie dog tore at a bone, the snowflakes melting into its oily coat. The Chief cursed under a van, then emerged rubbing his hands. He had a battered black stovepipe hat on his head and a face of scored leather. The children pushed a gig with uneven wheels and shouted in their singsong language. A baby squealed as the radio blared 'I shot a man in Reno just to watch him die'. They were there to stay, their territory marked by tar barrels.

In the nights I dreamed about them. The Chief scaled a grey crag with a blade between his teeth, scuttled like a lizard beneath the burning sun. Below in the canyon was the town, Lavery's Grocery, the broken pump and James Potter Victualler. Small dustclouds gathered in the streets, tumbleweed clutched the wheels of covered wagons. The Chief bared his teeth in a grin, slipped the blade into his pouch and was gone. The prairie dog strained at the leash as he approached across the plains, the heat shimmered in the cacti.

I stared open-mouthed at the hypnotic glow of the screen. There was nothing Audie Murphy could do. A gap-toothed renegade looped a rope across a branch and sneered 'It's a good day for a hanging, lawman'. Audie stood frozen as bleached bones stared up at him. 'If we hadn't gotten ya, them 'paches would have anyhow', said the renegade.

Somewhere behind the canyon ridge they lurked, moving on padded feet.

'Give me down the sugar', said Ma.

When I looked again, the renegade and his partners were on the ground staring out of dead eyes, Audie was galloping off on horseback with his hands tied behind his back and the Apaches were swarming like ants, the Chief standing above the dead men with an axe in his crossed hands.

'He steal from Apache, white man', he said, 'you lie, white-eyes'.

The renegade stared at the sky as a drum boomed.

The moon hung in a corner of the bedroom window as I heard Da and Jimmy the stonecutter stumbling on the gravel. Da coughed harshly and swore.

'Goodnight, Jimmy', I heard him say, 'I'll see you in The Vintage Christmas Eve.'

'Aye', Jimmy said.

I heard the door close and the sound of the holy picture falling in the hallway. Crockery rattled as she fixed his meal. Clouds trickled across the moon's face, a car passed in the darkness.

'You never were any different', I heard him say, 'whining from the day you were born.'

I saw her face in the ensuing silence, taut white skin, wounded eyes.

'Should have left you in that hole of a butcher shop. All you were good for.'

It went on far into the night. I heard the bedroom door close as the window glass paled and P. J. Masterson stared down the lane on his way to work.

'Sonofabitch', said Desie as we spied on them from the hill,' they haven't moved for an hour. She just sits there – like a stone.'

The black-faced children crawled in and out of a drainpipe. We sat there until evening and then Desie spat onto the grass and said: 'Move 'em out, pard'.'

We rode back into town on makebelieve colts.

We sat in the parlour listening to carols on the radio, its bead of light twinging in the half-darkness. Ma's needles clicked in time with the movement of the fireshadows. Da's lips moved in and out, he came out of a dream and said:

'Pete McDonald's not good. They say he won't see the Christmas.'

Ma shook her head and said nothing. He recalled a trip to Bundoran with Pete, hours spent climbing the cliffs in the hot sun.

'Nothing Pete didn't know about birds. A rare character. Wasn't a bird in the book he didn't know.'

Then he slipped away again, his fingers making tiny movements on the arm of the chair. A bird trotted along the garden wall. All you could hear was the sound of Ma's breathing.

'You travel long way?' said Desie as the Apache lad looked up at him with hunted eyes.

Desie pointed to himself.

'We', he said, accentuating his words, 'we – friends.'

The lad started back a little, watching our hands.

'We-live-in-town. You – Apache brave. You hear the spirit voices of dead warriors.'

The lad's face contorted. He stumbled, then ran off without looking back. Desie looked after him.

'He doesn't understand.'

The teepee was rigid, the ponies shuffled closer to the ditch for warmth. The squaw struggled through the snow with an enamel bucket to the frozen river. The radio played *Silver bells, silver bells, it's Christmas time in the city.*

There was a party in the house. A car pulled up outside and they came in singing, pulling off snowspeckled overcoats and heavy scarves. Jody Lennon and Charlie Keenan sang *South of the Border*. Glasses clinked and cigarette smoke filled the kitchen. Someone put on a 78 and they bagan to dance to the muted trumpets of the Inkspots.

'Will you ever forget them, Benny?', said Charlie to Da.

'Who do you know in heaven that made you the angel you are?' smiled Da, the whiskey tipping over the side of his glass.

After the dancing they sat for a long time around the fire talking about the old days and past Christmasses.

'This time last year, Harry was with us,' said Jody Lennon, 'poor Harry.'

'Who'd have thought it?', said Mrs McGirr, tapping her glass with thoughtful fingers.

'The time passes.'

'It does surely', they all agreed, 'it passes like that.'

The car engines revved up suddenly in the white night. Voices huddled together in the doorway as they gathered up gloves and hats.

'Please God we'll all be here this time next year.'

'I think she'll freeze.'

'Well a happy Christmas to one and all.'

'And many of them.'

They left then and all there was was the stark carpet of snow and the flakes in mad clusters around the amber streetlight.

Lying there in the darkness, I heard them talking. Ma was upset over something.

'I have my self-respect too', she said.

There were long silences. Then he said:

'You and your half-wit brother . . .'

'Why didn't you say that to his face? Why Benny?'

Their voices got louder. He shouted her down, then he cursed and I could hear her climbing out of bed. He called her back but she went downstairs. I could hear him dragging on the cigarette and the sound of the clock ticking as she sat by the fire downstairs. It was morning when her soft footsteps came hesitantly back up the stairs.

They were hardy because of all the winters they'd seen.

'He's like Crazy Horse', said Desie, nothing would ever break him.'

We drew pictures of him, an imposing shadow before the sun, feathered spear poised as he drew a bead on a rattler. The prairie stretched away lilke a sky. The squaw and him did not fight or argue. They had their own ways and they followed their code in silence. The longknives came to the Apache village. Rory Calhoun played The Chief. He bartered with the General, laid out rugs and wood carvings in the centre of the village. They shook hands. Rory bowed. But in the night, the longknives crept into the village like cats. They burnt the teepees to the ground and rounded up all the braves. They tied Calhoun to a tree and tortured him. They humiliated him in front of his squaw and the whole village. Then his head fell on his bloodstained chest, his black pigtails dangling. The General slapped his wrist with his white gloves and gestured to his men. They rode off and left the squaws to pick their way through the blackened ash of the burnt village.

'The bastards', cried Desie, 'the dirty bastards.'

We painted equals signs and arrows on our faces, sat parleying on orange boxes in the dimness of the deserted railway office. Desie pulled a rug around him and looked at me with wise, burrowing eyes as I explained why I had come to the village. He put on a deep voice and said:

'You come to the village of He-Who-Walks-The-World. We make you our brother.'

We mingled the blood of our wrists and then we smoked the pipe of peace. When it was finished, Desie looked out across the embankment and said:

'There's nothing else I want to be. I want to be one of them. They're free.'

'Yes', I said, thinking of them on a wide open trail, winding towards blue mountain valleys, 'Free.'

One day I came home and found Ma crying over the sink. She just kept picking at the dishes with the tears coming down her face. I went white, I did not know what to do. I stood there not knowing whether to touch her or run out. She half-looked at me and struggled for words:

'I don't know why it happens, son . . . he was never bitter . . . some day I'll tell you . . . you wouldn't understand yet . . . .'

She kept talking in muddled sentences about other times – a boarding house in Bundoran, a day at the Giant's Causeway, all about a time I knew nothing about. I stood there in silence, the hard frosted sun slanting in through the window, trying to make sense of what she said. It seemed like years passed as we stood there, a chainsaw drilling in the distance.

At night the orange camp fire flickered, its tarry smoke filling the air. Odd times Apaches came from camps far away, crept in like ghosts and sat around in a circle. Their hair was thick and black, ropes around their waists. You could see their touch, creased faces moving in and out of the light. Dead rabbits hung from a branch. The prairie dog's vigilant snout sat on its paws. Sometimes they sang in low voices, a deep penetrating hum that spread outwards like a fanning claw.

'They're calling to the spirits of the happy hunting grounds', said Desie.

'The Manitou', I said, 'they're praying to The Manitou.'

'Jesus', said Desie, as we slipped back behind the hill into the darkness,' The Manitou.'

Christmas day the place was a ghost town. Beer trails from the night before froze on the sidewalk outside the bars, the grocery sign creaked relentlessly. In the evening Desie and me went tracking in The Hairy Mountains, trudging over crusted hoof-holes in search of badger's imprints with our staffs in hand. When I got home the doors were locked. There was no answer, it seemed the house was deserted. I managed to prise the scullery window open with my penknife. In the kitchen embers glowed in the fire. I got the feeling of being in a strange world. In the half-light their picture looked down at me. She was wearing a wide-brimmed hat with a flower, her white handbag hanging from her arm. Behind them a poster *King's Hall Belfast – Gracie Fields – Jan. 10 1953*. The fire glinted in the brass ornaments on the mantelpiece, behind the clock memoriam cards and bound letters going back a long time, a photograph of uncle Joe in a summer hayfield. I stood there without moving, I did not know what to say about these things. Then I heard a sort of moan. I tensed and whispered 'Who is it?' but no answer came. For no reason I thought of a stalking hunter in a wolfskin. I crept slowly up the stairs then

I heard it again. It was coming from their room. I bent and through the keyhole the image meant nothing to me at first, it was an optical puzzle that came slowly into focus. It was his back, marked with the startling whiteness of age. It moved up and down rhythmically. He groaned. I heard Ma, she seemed to be in pain. She kept saying 'Please, please'. For a long time they were like this. Then Da eased downward. There was silence. Then I could hear her sobs. Da turned away on his side.

'Why Benny?', she said, 'What happened Benny? Please . . . tell me . . . .'

He did not answer. The silence seemed to swell up and fill up the room like a balloon.

The sky slowly inked itself in. The snow began again, in the distance the lights went out in the town. I lit a fire in the deserted office and burnt old papers and files discarded from the days of the railway. There were still posters on the walls, left from the days Ma and Da had first come to the town to live. A couple in old-fashioned clothes stood smiling with their suitcases, behind them the fading outline of London's Tower Bridge. Outside the Hairy Mountains rose up like black tidal waves. When the fire died I sat there thinking but everything was twisted in my head. I saw her smiling in an olden days café with wooden booths and weak-coloured advertisements. I saw her turn away as his parchment-like body heaved above her, felt the taut silence of the kitchen as we sat there under the drowsy spell of he kitchen, the days it brought back melting almost as they came. I could not hold any of the thoughts long enough to make anything of them, they dissipated like smoke and then converged under a new image. I kicked over the ashes of the fire and went out. There was no sound as

I walked, the snow took my steps and made silence of them. For a long time I strode, through the hunting grounds of winter, thinking how there would be dead buffalo in the mountains. I kept saying the name to myself, it was the only thing kept me going He-Who-Walks-The-World. There was still a tiny coil of smoke coming from the fire when I got there. I could hear The Chief snoring in the teepee. The pony pawed the dirt. I crept past the prairie dog and he didn't stir. I clung to what was left of the fire but the frost edged into my whole body, I could not stop shivering. When I looked up The Chief was standing there with a blanket around him. His long black hair half-covered his craggy face.

'He-Who-Walks-The-World', I said.

'Yes', he said, his voice deep, commanding.

After that everything seemed to move slowly before my eyes, a rabbit turned slowly over the fire, the blackfaced children stared with their fingers in their mouths, the squaw held out bread to me without speaking. The Chief and I ate together. He sat with his legs crossed and I felt his eyes inside me. The smoke curled and the snow fell hypnotically. We seemed to sit there for hours until I felt myself drifting across a vast plain where the sun beat down relentlessly on the red powdery sand. There came sounds of movement, of faces without shape gathering bundles and sending smokeclouds up from a fire as animals were made ready to press south to the fertile valleys now that the white men had killed all the buffalo, Rory Calhoun taking a last look at the settlers' cabins that now dotted his terrain, before waving to his gathered people and setting off into the night. Then I fell away again, tumbling above the plain like dust.

When I came to, they were gone, it was as if they had never been there. In the distance I saw Desie and

Da on the hill. I waited, watching the snow covering their tracks. Desie hung back uncertainly. Da was white, he did not know what to say.

'They're gone, Desie', I said.

Da's eyes darted between us.

'Yes', said Desie.

'They had to Desie', I said, 'The Longknives.'

Da stood looking at me. 'You should have told us son', he said, 'anything could have happened. You don't know those people.'

I nodded. I didn't feel anything about it now. We said nothing more, just stood there for a long time as the snow blew in clouds towards the town where Ma stood waiting by the window, oblivious of their soundless passage through the deserted streets, in the kitchen's shadows.

THE JOURNEY TO SOMEWHERE ELSE

ANNE DEVLIN

The snowroad to the Alps runs south-east from Lyons to Chambéry whereafter, leaving the autoroute behind, it takes up with a steep mountain road north to Mégrève on the western slopes of Mont Blanc.

The resort café, several miles above the village, was full of seventeen-year-old French millionaires – or so it seemed to us – and large Italian families: the women wore fur hats with their ski-suits and too many rings for comfort; their men had paunches and smoked cigars at lunch; and the twelve-year-old Italian girls confirmed for all time that fourteen was the only age to marry and Capulet's daughter might never have been such a catch had she lived long enough to look like her mother. There were probably some large French families as well, but they were less inclined to sit together as a group. The resort on the borders with Switzerland and Italy was fairly cosmopolitan; confirming too that the rich, like their money, are not different but indifferent to frontiers. Whatever nation they came from, they had nannies for their children, who cut up the food at different tables and did not ski. On Christmas Day opposite me a black woman peeled a small orange and fed it to a fat white child, piece by piece. The smell did it: Satsumas!

Christmas Day in '59; they ran the buses in Belfast; the

pungent smell of orange brought it back. My brother, the satsumas in green and red silver paper on the piano in the parlour, the fire dying in the grate and the adults asleep in their rooms. And that year, in '59 when I was eight, it had begun to snow. The grate-iron to rest the kettle on squeaked as I pushed it towards the coals with my foot.

'You'll burn your slipper soles,' Michael John said.

'I'm bored.'

'We could go out.'

'How?'

'The bus passes to the City Hall every fifteen minutes.'

'They'll not allow us. I've no money and – '

'Ah go on, Amee. I dare you,' he said. 'Run out, catch the next bus to the City Hall and come back up on it without paying.'

'But the conductor will put me off!'

'That's the dare. See how far you can get. The person who gets furthest wins!'

My brother was small and fair and mischievous; there was ten months' difference in our ages.

'All right then, I'll go.'

Joe is dark and tall and mostly silent; there is ten years between us.

'Would you like me to get one for you?' Joe said, putting the lunch tray on the table in front of me. 'Amee, would you like one?'

'What?'

'The oranges you keep staring at,' he said, handing me a glass of cold red wine.

'I'm sorry. No. I don't really like them very much.'

'You're shivering.'

'The wine's so cold.'

'Grumble. Grumble.'

112

'I'm sorry.'

With the life in the room the windows in the café clouded over.

'It would help if you stopped breathing,' he joked, as the window next to us misted.

It was a doomed journey from the start. Like all our holidays together, it was full of incidents, mishaps and narrow escapes. Once, in Crete, I nearly drowned. I fell off his mother's boyfriend's boat and swallowed too much water. I remember coming up for air and watching him staring at me from the deck; he had been a lifesaver on a beach one summer, but I swam to those rocks myself. Four years ago in Switzerland, where he was working at the time, I fell on a glacier mountain, the Jungfrau, and slid headlong towards the edge with my skis behind me. I screamed for several minutes before I realized that if I continued to panic I would probably break my neck. I stopped screaming and thought about saving myself. At which point everything slowed down and I turned my body round on the snow, put my skis between me and the icy ridge and came to a halt. When I had enough energy I climbed back up. I suppose what happened this time was inevitable. About an hour after we crossed the Channel he crashed the car in Béthune. He drove at speed into the back of the one in front. I saw the crash coming and held my breath. On the passenger side we ended up minus a headlamp and with a very crumpled wing.

'Why didn't you shout if you saw it coming?' he objected later.

'It seemed a waste of energy,' I said. 'I couldn't have prevented it happening.'

We exchanged it for a French car at Arrais and after I travelled apprehensively towards the Alps.

'Why don't we ski separately?' I suggested, after the first week. 'I'd like some ski lessons. Anyway, you're a far more advanced skier. I only hold you back.'

On the second day of that week I came back from ski class at four thirty and waited for him in the café by the main telecabin. There were so few people inside now the glass was almost clear. A family group sat at one table and the ski instructors at the bar drank cognac. I waited for half an hour before I noticed the time.

It was snowing heavily outside then as well, and even getting dark. The snow was turning blue in the light. I closed the heavy front door behind me lightly till the snib caught and ran across the road to wait at the stop. I could see him watching at the lace curtains in the sitting room. The Christmas-tree lights were on in the room, the curtain shifted. Soundlessly, the bus arrived. I got on, and just as quietly it moved off. The conductor was not on the platform, nor was he on the lower deck, so I went to the front and crouched low on the seat and hoped he wouldn't notice me when he did appear. There was no one else aboard but two old ladies in hats with shopping baskets and empty Lucozade bottles. Noisily, the conductor came downstairs. He stood on the platform clinking small change; I could see his reflection in the glass window of the driver's seat. If I was lucky he would not bother me, I was too far away from the platform. Suddenly, he started to walk up the bus. I looked steadfastly out of the window. He rapped the glass pane to the driver and said something. The driver nodded. He spoke again. I was in such terror of a confrontation that I didn't hear anything he said. For a moment he glanced in my direction, and he remained where he stood. We were nearing the cinemas at the end of the road. At this point I decided not to go all the way round the route to the City Hall. I got up quickly and walked down the bus away from him and stood uneasily on the platform. At the traffic lights before the proper stop, he moved along the bus towards me, my nerve failed and I leaped off.

'Hey!' he called out. 'You can't get off here.'

It was snowing more heavily. Wet snow. My feet were cold. I looked down and saw that I was still wearing my slippers; red felt slippers with a pink fur trim. How strange I must have looked in a duffel coat and slippers in the snow. The clock of the Presbyterian Assembly Buildings read five forty-five. It chimed on the quarter-hour, and behind me the lights of a closed-up confectioner's illuminated a man I had not noticed before. 'You'll get your nice slippers wet,' he said.

'I'll dry them when I get home,' I said.

'You'll get chilblains that way.'

'No I won't.'

I looked doubtfully at my slippers; the red at the toes was darker than the rest and my feet felt very uncomfortable.

'Have you far to walk when you get off the bus?' he asked.

'No. I live just up the road. The bus passes my house,' I said.

'You'd better stand in here. It's drier,' he said.

I didn't answer. At that moment a young woman came round the corner into view and began walking towards us from the town centre. She walked with difficulty through the snow in high shoes. Under her coat a black dress and white apron showed as she moved. The woman looked at me and then at the man and stopped. She drew a packet of cigarettes from her apron pocket and lit one. At first she waited at the stop with me, and then, shivering, moved back into the protective shelter of the shop front by the man's side.

'That wind 'ud go clean through you so it would,' she said.

'Aye. It comes in off the Lough and goes straight up the Black Mountain,' he said, looking away up the road. The woman and I followed his gaze.

Beyond us, a block or two away, was the dolls' hospital, we had been there a few weeks before with my mother.

'Leave the aeroplanes alone, Michael John!' she scolded. 'Just wait and see what Santa brings you.'

I loved that shop with all its dolls, repaired, redressed. My own doll had started out from there as a crinoline lady in white net with hoops and red velvet bows. That year, when we left it at the shop minus a leg it had been returned to me as a Spanish dancer in a petticoat of multicoloured layers. We only ever visited the town with my mother; during the day when it was busy and friendly, when the matinées at the cinema were going in and the traffic moved round the centre, the cinema confectioner's shop in front of which I stood was always open and sold rainbow drops and white chocolate mice – the latter turned up in my stocking – so were there too, I noticed for the first time, satsumas in that window.

The snow, and the quiet and the darkness had transformed the town. In the blue-grey light the charm of the life went out of it, it seemed unfamiliar, dead. I wanted to go home to the fire in the parlour; I began to shiver convulsively, and then the bus came.

'Ardoyne.' The woman looked out. 'That's my bus.'

I was so grateful I forgot about the dare.

'No good to you?' she said to the man.

He shook his head and pulled up the collar of his coat.

'Merry Christmas,' she called out as we got on.

I was sitting brazenly at the seat next to the platform when the conductor turned to me for the fare.

'I forgot my purse,' I said. 'But this bus passes my house, my Mammy'll pay it when I get home.'

'Oh your Mammy'll pay it when you get home!' he mimicked. 'Did you hear that now!'

The young woman, who had gone a little further up the bus, turned round. We had only moved a couple of streets beyond the shop, the toyshop was behind me. A wire cage encased its shop front.

'Please don't put me off now,' I said, beginning to cry.

'I'll pay her fare,' the young woman said.

'Does your Mammy know you're out at all?' he asked and, getting no answer moved along to the woman. 'Where are you going to anyway?' he called back.

'The stop before the hospital stop,' I said weakly.

'The Royal,' he said to the woman. The ticket machine rolled once.

'And Ardoyne. The terminus,' she said.

The ticket machine rolled once more and they grumbled between them about having to work on Christmas Day.

'I'll be late getting my dinner tonight. Our ones'll all have finished when I get in.'

'Aye sure I know. I'm not off till eight,' he said. 'It's hardly been worth it. The one day in the year.' He snapped the tickets off the roll and gave her the change. 'And no overtime.'

Someone, a man, clambered downstairs to the platform. He had a metal tin under his arm. The conductor pulled the bell.

'No overtime? You're kiddin',' she said.

'That's the Corporation for you,' he said.

117

Before the hospital stop he pulled the bell again. I stepped down to the platform. I could see the Christmas-tree lights in the bay window of the parlour. I jumped off and ran towards the house, and wished that I hadn't been too ashamed to thank her. But her head was down and she wasn't looking after me.

Michael John opened the door: 'You did it?' he said, half in awe. 'I saw you get off the bus. You did it!'

'Yes,' I gasped. My heart was pounding and my feet hurt.

'All the way to the City Hall?'

'Of course.'

He followed me into the parlour.

'But look at your slippers, Amee, they're ruined. You went out in your slippers. They'll know.'

'Not if I dry them. No one will ever know.'

I put my slippers on the fender and stood looking at the red dye on the toes of my white tights. I pulled off the stockings as well and saw that even my toes were stained.

'Look at that, Michael John! My toes are dyed!' I said. 'Michael John?'

The front door closed so quietly it was hardly audible.

'Michael John! Don't go!'

From the sitting-room window I could see him crossing the road.

'Oh I only pretended,' I breathed. 'I didn't.'

But he was too far away. And then the bus came.

I waited at that window until my breathing clouded the glass. I rubbed it away with my fist. Every now and then I checked the slippers drying at the fender. Gradually the dark red faded, the toes curled up and only a thin white line remained. I went back to the window and listened for the bus returning. Several buses did come by, but Michael John did not. I got under the velvet drapes and the lace and stood watching at the glass where the cold is trapped and waited. I would tell him the truth when he came back. The overhead lights of the sitting room blazed on and my mother's voice called:

'Ameldia! What are you doing there?'

She looked crossly round the room.

'You've even let the fire go out! Where is Michael John?'

'Excusez-moi? Madame Fitzgerald?' the witress in the café asked.

My ski pass lay on the table, she glanced at it briefly; the photograph and the name reassured her.

'Telephone!' she said, indicating that I should follow.

The ski instructors at the bar turned their heads to watch as I passed by to the phone. They were the only group left in the café. I expected to hear Joe's voice, instead a woman at the other end of the line spoke rapid French.

'Please. Could you speak English?' I asked.

She repeated her message.

'Your friend is here at the clinic in the village. We have X-rayed him. He will now return to your hotel. Can you please make your own way back.'

'Yes. But what is wrong?'

'I'm sorry?'

'What is wrong with him?'

'An accident. Not serious.'

'Thank you,' I said, and hurried away from the phone.

Outside it was dark and still snowing. I knew two routes back to the village: there was the mountain route we had skied down on after class a few days before, half an hour earlier by the light; and there was the route by road which we had driven up on in the morning. I could also take the bus. It was five twenty. The lifts and telecabins closed nearly an hour before. The bus which met the end of ski class had long gone; so too had the skiers to the town. The only people left seemed to be resort staff and instructors, most of whom lived on the mountain. It took five minutes to ski down to the village on the mountain and forty-five minutes to go by road – if a bus came. Without further hesitation I made the decision to take the shortest route back. It was too dark to ski, so I put my skis on my shoulder and started out to walk along the ski-track down the mountain.

I followed the path confidently at first, encouraged by the sight of three young men who were walking fairly swiftly ahead. Half-way down the hill through a farm, which even in deep snow smelt of farming, I passed a woman, going in the opposite direction, who looked at me briefly and said:

'Bonsoir, madame.'

The surprise in her voice and the weight of the skis on my shoulder arrested me momentarily so I stopped: 'Bonsoir.'

I shifted the skis to my other shoulder and in so doing realized that I had lost sight of the walkers ahead. I walked on to a turning point by a chalet and found there that the path forked two ways. There was no one ahead anymore, and looking back uphill I found that the woman had disappeared. The lights of the village twinkled before me, directly below the treeline, luring me down the slope. The other path stretched more gradually down around the mountain. In the light it had been so easy. I stood for a moment staring at the mute grey wetness. Were there really two tracks? The longer I stood in the dark looking, the more confusing it became. If I don't move now it will be too late. I moved. I set off again rapidly downhill, but the weight of the skis on my shoulder and the slippery gradient propelled me onwards at a hair-raising speed towards the treeline. The hard plastic boots made it impossible to grip the snow. I slipped badly and then stopped suddenly against the slope. My legs shook. I was breathless. If I moved another inch I would probably break a leg. Lost. I'm lost as well. If I could only be sure that this was the right way. Perhaps the wider more gradual path is the one. I set off to climb back to the fork again. A light in the chalet further up the slope reassured me. I could always ask there.

Breathless, I regained the beginning of the two paths. I did not approach the chalet, but set out confidently on the wider path. The route ran between the snowdrifts higher on the mountain side than on the valley, but I saw also that now I was leaving the lights of the village behind, and this path, although easier to follow, was leading directly into a wood of pines above me. I came to a small grotto on the valley side of the slope, and beyond, a little further up on the mountain, I could see the white, stone façade of a closed church. A mound of snow nestling uneasily on the steep roof of the grotto slid off quietly in slow motion into my path, seconds before I reached it. Perversely I plundered on. This is the wrong way, I'm sure it is, I thought. More precious energy sapped by the extra effort of wading through the drift I came once more to a halt. The wind blew relentlessly. I noticed it for the first time. There is something noxious about the innocence of snow in its insidious transformation of familiar routes. I must go back. I turned and hurried back between the church and grotto, and reached, with a great deal of effort, the turning point on the path yet again. If I meet someone now will they be friend or foe? If I go to that chalet to ask will I be welcome? If I could somehow find the energy to climb further. I suddenly understood more perfectly than at any other moment that Fate, like a love affair, is a matter of timing: the right person passing at the right time; a combination of moments from experience which coming round like a memory, recurring, inducing in us the same confusion. It was as though I had stood all my life in the same cold place between the curtain and the glass. How stupid I am. This whole journey is pointless, I said aloud to no one. I could have gone for the bus. I closed my eyes and breathed painfully.

'Where is Michael John, Ameldia? Why did you let him go? You're older, you should be more responsible! What bus? At what time?'

The conductor remembered him. He didn't have any money. No, he didn't put him off. On Christmas Day for thrupence? It wasn't worth it. He didn't remember when he got off. He hadn't seen him get off. There was a memorial service on the feast of the Purification; they waited and waited. There was no coffin, only flowers in the church, and my mother's tears all during the service. He went away so completely, he even went out of my dreams. Fair and small and mischievous.

When I opened my eyes a white mist was forming. I would have to hurry and get to the road before it enveloped me completely. Every step uphill was excruciatingly painful as again and again the skis bit into my shoulder. As I neared the top of the hill, passing through the farm smells, I heard voices. Two girls and a boy appeared, I went very slowly passing them higher up the slope; I had climbed very high. They took the downward path, several feet of snow separated us. They did not glance in my direction and I had lost my curiosity about the route. We passed in silence. I got to the road again where I started out, exhausted. Did anyone pass him that night and not know?

Once on the highway I walked more easily where the traffic of the day had beaten down the snowtrack. My alarm had evaporated like the mist on the mountain. But I was hungry and tired and when I reached the car-park where the ski bus turned it was deserted, no one was waiting. I put the skis into a bank of snow and lay against them. My face burned, and my hair clung to my forehead from the effort and panic of climbing. A car passed. It was too dark to read my watch. If I walked on to the road towards the lights I would be able to read the time. I was too tired to move. My shoulders ached: I could not lift my arms above my head. My clothes clung. The backs of my knees were damp. My leather gloves looked swollen and bloated. Another car passed. It must be late; perhaps he will come out looking for me. If I go and stand on the road he might see me. I was too weary to move, so I stayed on. Then a familiar throaty rattle of an engine sounded, and a bus turned into the coach-park.

'Mégève?'

'Non. Sallandes.'

'Oh.' I must have looked disappointed.

'Dix minutes!' he assured me.

'Oh. Merci, monsieur!' I brightened.

He was back in half the time to pick me up. I dropped my skis into the cage at the back and in a few minutes we were hurtling down the mountain towards the village.

At seven thirty I got to the hotel. Joe was not there. The X-rays from the clinic were lying on the bed.

Perhaps he was worried and has gone out looking for me, I thought. I was drying my wet clothes on the radiators when he came in.

'What on earth happened?' I asked at the sight of the sling.

'Oh, some idiot got out of control and jumped on my back this afternoon. Arrogant lout. He didn't even apologize. He said I shouldn't have stopped suddenly in front of him.'

'Why did you stop?'

'A girl in front of me fell down. I stopped to help her.'

'It's dangerous though, isn't it. You should have skied round her to safety and then stopped.'

'Well, anyway, I won't be able to ski again this holiday,' he said. 'The ligaments are torn.'

'Is it very painful?'

'It's a bit sore.'

'I'm sorry. Shall we go back tomorrow?'

'Well, we could go to Paris tomorrow instead of on Friday.'

'Let's do that, I'll drive,' I said.

'There's no need. I can manage. I have no trouble driving' he said. 'How are you then, all right? Had a nice day?'

'Joe, I got lost on the mountaqin.'

'Did you?' he said 'Oh, by the way, I've been downstairs talking to Madame. I told her that we were leaving earlier. She was very sympathetic when she saw the sling. She said she wouldn't charge us for thie extra nights even though we've booked to stay till Friday.'

'I tried to walk down the path we skied on and then I couldn't find it.'

'That was silly,' he said. 'Why didn't you get the bus?'

'I don't know.'

It wasn't the first time in our ten-year relationship of living together and not living together that I found I had nothing to tell him. He never guesed the fury of my drama; and now he looked pale and tired.

'What's the matter?' he asked, catching me watching him.

'Nothing. Nothing's the matter.'

Even in Montmartre there was snow and coldness.

'There's a hotel! Stop now!' I said.

We had been driving all day, yet it seemed as though we never left the snowline.

'Stop! Please. The hotel looked nice. Joe, I'm not navigating a street further.'

'Ameldia, it's a five-star hotel!' he said, in a voice that reminded me of my mother. 'We are not staying in a five-star hotel!'

'It's on me,' I said extravagantly. 'Whatever this costs, it's on me!'

'But Amee, you don't have any money!'

'I'll argue with the bank manager about that, not with you,' I said. 'I have a little plastic card here which will settle everything. Now will you get out of the car. Please Joe. You look exhausted!'

We signed into a fourth-floor side room. Through the nylon curtains I could see the traffic of Paris and the lights of the Eiffel Tower. 'We can walk to the Sacré Coeur from here. I think I remember the way,' I said.

My last visit had been as a schoolgirl fifteen years before.

There were tangerines in the restaurant – I lifted my head to them as they passed on the fruit tray to the table next to us – and ice-cubes on the grapes. I shivered involuntarily. I don't remember satsumas any other year.

'I forgot to ring my mother on Christmas Day!' I said suddenly.

'From the French Alps? Why would you want to do that?' he said.

'You know what they're like about my being away for Christmas.'

'No, I'm afraid I don't, I've never met them,' he said firmly. 'And I'm afraid I don't see why you think they should still be so obsessed with you. You are thirty years of age now, Ameldia, and you do have other brothers and sisters!'

'Yes, I know. But I was the only one around when–'

'Forget it!' he said 'I didn't spend all this money and bring you all this way for you to drag that up now!'

'Madame? Monsieur?' A waiter stood eyeing us, his pencil poised like a dagger ready to attack his notepad.

Later as we passed through the square in Montmartre sad-eyed artists were putting their easels away. An African spread out ivory bangles and elephants on a cloth on the pavement and I stopped to admire. He spoke English: 'Are you English?'

'No. Irlande.'

'Ah. Irlande is good,' he said, putting an arm around me and drawing me towards his wares. I felt like a schoolgirl again, shy, drawing away, explaining I had no money to buy anything.

Joe watched me from a distance and I said: 'Don't be so grumpy.'

'I'm not grumpy,' he said crossly.

'Wouldn't it be nice to go and have a glass of wine in one of those bars,' I said.

'Well, they look very crowded to me and I'm tired,' he said.

'Do you know why I love Montmartre?'

126

'No, but I'm sure you're going to tell me!' he said.

'Because whatever time you come here, it's always open, full of people.'

I wished I hadn't brought him to Montmartre. He seemed so uneasy amidst the haggle of trading in the streets. I had forgotten how he hated markets. He did not relax until we got back to the hotel.

I was not tired and didn't find that sleep came easily. My tossing and turning kept him awake.

'Where did you get that cough from?' he asked.

'I must have got cold somewhere.'

I got up and went to the fridge for a glass of mineral water and as I opened the door in the dark, I thought I smelt oranges.

'Did you spill the fruit juice?' I asked.

'No,' he said wearily. 'When will you go to sleep?'

I went to the shower room to drink the water so as not to disturb him and when I returned to the bedroom I found it was very much colder than when I'd left it. The curtain shifting slightly caught my attention. The glass in the window was so clear it looked as if it wasn't there at all.

'Joe?' I called softly. 'Did you open the window?'

'No,' he said without stirring.

The room appeared to be filling with a white mist. It's like on the mountain, I thought. The white mist of the night outside seemed to grow into the room.

'That's funny.' The smell of oranges was very strong. 'Somebody is eating satsumas!' I said aloud.

Joe didn't answer. I got into bed and lay down trembling. The walls of the room were gradually slipping away to the mist. 'No. I will not watch,' I said firmly. 'I will not watch any more.' I closed my eyes tight against the dark and breathed softly.

Where the white rocks of the Antrim Plateau meet the mud banks of the Lough, three small boys netting crabs dislodged a large stone, when one of them reaching into the water after the escaping crab caught instead the cold hand of my brother. In May a closed coffin filled the sitting room and the Children of Mary from the neighbourhood came to pray there and keep the vigil.

'I will not watch,' I said. 'I will not watch.'

An angel of Portland stone marked the grave and we sang: 'Blood of my Saviour wash me in thy tide'. 'He was bound for heaven,' my mother said often, and that seemed to console her. And every Sunday of the year we went to the cemetery, my mother and I; on Christmas Day ever after we left offerings of flowers and things until even the angelstone aged, became pockmarked and turned brown. It was the first Christmas I had not gone to that grave.

In the morning Joe drew back the curtains in the room and said: 'What a sight! I'm glad I didn't know that was there last night.'

'Didn't know what?' I said, moving to the window.

'Look!'

A huddle of stone crucifixes, headstones and vaults marked the graves which jostled for the space under our window against the side wall of the hotel.

'Montmartre cemetery!' he said.

There were no angels among the headstones.

'How creepy! Well, I'm glad we're going,' he said, with a last glance before dropping the curtain.

But I could still see.

'Last night,' I began to say, 'this room was very cold and I asked you if – '

'Oh, do come away from the window and hurry up and pack,' he said. 'We need to catch the lunch-time ferry.'

I wanted to tell him what I knew, that the future was already a part of what I was becoming, and if I stopped this becoming there would be no future only an endless repetition of moments from the past which I will be compelled to relive. 'It would help if you stopped breathing,' he had said. But it wouldn't; because there would always be the memory of existence – like a snare; a trapped moment, hungover in the wrong time. Unaccountable. And I wanted to tell him before it was too late that the difference is as fragile between the living and the dead as the absence of breath on a glass. But already he was rushing on a journey to somewhere else.

Bound for heaven, was it? Yes. Hand and foot.

FINEGAN'S ARK

JAMES PLUNKETT

I t was while he was pushing his way through the
Christmas crowds in Moore Street, Finegan told
us, he remembered the Noah's Ark the Granny
and the Aunt had bought him in the self-same street
well over 40 Christmas Eves before.

It was a sudden and vivid memory, he said – the
kind that hits you in some vital part of the machinery
and makes everything grind to a stop. Did we ever
experience anything of that kind?

Joe left down his glass to say he had. I did the same
and said I knew what he meant. Casey avoided
comment by picking flakes of cigarette ash out of his
whiskey with the help of a pencil. A stout man and a
nondescript kind of a man with a muffler whom none
of us knew leaned over from their table in the corner
and listened carefully.

Apart from the two strangers at the table there were
only the four of us in the Snug. Normally we would
have been in the bar, but what the Boss called 'The
Grand Xmas Draw' was to take place that night and
this year the four of us had been selected to draw out
the tickets and to ensure that all was conducted in
accordance with the requirements of justice and fair
play.

It was the custom on Christmas Eve to segregate
those so honoured from the riff-raff in the public bar.
Why, I don't know – perhaps as a precaution against
corruption and malpractice and to lend dignity and a
sense of occasion. Anyway, there we all were, waiting

for the Boss himself to give us the word that everything was in readiness.

'When I looked around,' Finegan said, continuing with his Epiphany, 'dammit if everything wasn't exactly the same as on that evening 40 years ago.'

Then he went on to describe the scene: the fog under the lamps, the thronging people, the carol singers shaking their collection boxes and the traders with barrows jamming both sides of the street, all bawling out their novelties under a forest of balloons. It was a very affecting description.

'I like carol singers,' the stout man told us. 'When I hear the carol singers I do get a lump in my throat.'

'What class of an Ark was it?' Joe asked.

'a wooden one,' Finegan said, 'with a figure of Noah and a collection of animals to go with it.'

'That's a nice gift for a child,' the stout man approved. 'I believe in gifts that encourage a fitting respect for our holy religion in the child.'

Casey, I noticed, looked across at him sourly, but then Casey was looking sourly at practically everything bar his whiskey that night, so nobody minded.

'I remember asking the shopkeeper would it float,' Finegan continued, 'and he told me it would and he patted me on the head.'

'That was for the benefit of the Granny and the Aunt,' Casey put in.

'I think that was very nice,' Joe said getting soft, 'an Ark that floated.'

But Finegan shook his head and said that that was the ugly part of it – that he was coming to. After five minutes in a bathtub the joints had opened and Ark and animals had gone to the bottom.

Noah had floated a bit longer than the rest, he told us. And then he described Noah lying on his back staring up at him with saucer-blue eyes, unable to believe that God had let him down.

Joe was astounded.

'That'd shake your faith in anything,' he said.

'There's terrible rogues and liars loose in the world,' the stout man said. And for the first and last time that night the man in the muffler took his nose out of his hot rum.

'A poor little child,' he said, unable to believe it.

Then the Boss brought more drink to us and said everything would be ready very soon. The pair in the corner had more hot rum and the stout man, remarking the notice of 'The Grand Xmas Draw' on the wall, said he'd like a ticket for that and the Boss sold him one. Casey gave him another sour look and turned to Finegan.

'I didn't know the Granny was a Protestant,' he remarked.

Finegan was astounded.

'The Granny was no bloody Protestant,' he said, putting his glass down to bang the table, 'and I'd like to know who's spreading a rumour like that about me and mine.'

'In the name of God,' Joe said to Casey, scenting a row, 'what made you say a thing like that?'

'It struck me that a Noah's Ark is a very Protestant class of a toy – that's all,' Casey said, very coolly, I thought.

At that moment, by good fortune, the Boss arrived in with more drink, which had a soothing effect on everybody, especially the stout man, who now butted in to mollify all concerned.

'Let's all remember it's the Eve of Christmas,' he said, 'and listen to that lovely singing there outside.'

There were tears in his eyes. The sound of a carol drifted in and when I looked around I saw silhouettes against the frosted glass. The smaller figures, the children, held candles that flickered behind cardboard shields. Looked at through the glass, each flame wore a nimbus.

It made Joe remember in his turn going down Moore Street as a child. It was the Granny and the Mammy he used to go with he told us – God be good to them, for they were both long since in their clay.

'I remember often enough,' he said, 'standing outside the public-house waiting for them. I knew well enough they were in there coaxing themselves to a couple of hot clarets on the sly, but of course – so as not to give scandal or bad example – they used to pretend to me that they were short taken.'

Casey looked up at heaven. The stout man lowered a man-sized mouthful of the rum and said that it only went to show what a shining thing Irish Catholic motherhood could be, and that Christmas, when all was said and done, was really a time for the children.

He used to sing in the Church choir himself at Midnight mass, he said, which was the happiest days of his life. Where would a man be without his Irish mother and the comforts of God's Holy Religion. We all agreed with him.

'Listen to that, for instance,' he said, pointing a finger at the ceiling.

We listened. It was shaking under the weight of scores of merrymakers in the upstairs lounge.

'The majority up there,' he said, 'is young blades getting parlatic on the smell of a cork, the holly and ivy drinkers out of our so-called Catholic university. Not to mention the young bits of girls with them, that should be at home helping the mammy to stuff the turkey and wash the kids for early Mass in the morning.'

'Ah, now,' Joe said reasonably, 'suffer the young. Sure we're only young once.'

'I agree with our friend,' Finegan said severely. 'If they were daughters of mine it's sore bottoms they'd all have. That's what they'd suffer from.'

Then the Boss himself came in with another drink and said that all was in readiness for the draw. So Joe raised the glass to everybody and said: 'Well, here's a happy Christmas.'

'A happy Christmas,' we all said.

'With knobs on,' Casey said, and glared again at the stout man.

We trooped up the stairs. A large box full of raffle tickets stood in the centre of the Boss's sitting-room and about it were set out the prizes – turkeys, hams, bottles of whiskey, port and sherry, packets of cigarettes, rich Christmas cakes, boxes of chocolates.

We began the draw, and of course the inevbitable happened. The first ticket out was number 445 and we all remembered it belonged to the stout man.

'There's the luck of the draw for you now,' Joe said. 'We're drinking here all the year round and a stranger comes along and has the coolness to win first prize.'

'He has,' Casey said, 'and do you know who that stranger is?'

'A Protestant, no doubt,' Finegan said, his resentment flaring up again.

'Whoever he is,' Joe said peaceably, 'he's a decent poor divil anyway, with a nice, natural upbringing. Did you see the way he cried when he heard the children singing the carols?'

'Let me tell you who he is,' Casey said, glaring at him. 'He's a notorious bloody receiver of stolen articles – a fence. And that skinny little gurrier with him is just out of the gaol after a sentence for burglary.'

Casey works in the courts, delivering summonses and all that class of thing, so none of us dared to doubt him. The Boss got pale.

'Merciful God,' he said, 'ruined.'

We all understood what he meant. If it got noised abroad that fences and burglars were taking to frequenting his premises in such numbers that they won prizes in his Grand Xmas Draw it would do his business no good in the world. It was a time for swift decisions. Casey looked at the Boss, then at us. Without a word he took ticket number 445 and tore it up.

'Is that agreed, boys?' he asked.

We all nodded. There was no need to ask what he meant.

'Right,' Casey said, 'now, in the name of God, let's start the draw.'

When it was over we went back to the bar and certified that everything had been done in strict accord with honesty and fair play and we announced the results. We returned to the Snug again for more drink, this time on the house. The Boss had one with us and so had Muffler and the stout man.

The carol singers outside began again. The stout man wept copiously, so that the tears splashed into his hot rum. Casey, raising his glass, gave us a toast.

'Here's to Noah,' he said, staring hard at Finegan. I looked into my glass and saw two unbelieving, saucer-blue eyes.

A PRESENT FOR CHRISTMAS

BERNARD MacLAVERTY

McGettigan woke in the light of midday, numb with the cold. He had forgotten to close the door the night before and his coat had slipped off him onto the boards of the floor. He swivelled round on the sofa and put the overcoat on, trying to stop shivering. At his feet there was a dark green wine bottle and his hand shook as he reached out to test its weight. He wondered if he had had the foresight to leave a drop to warm himself in the morning. It was empty and he flung it in the corner with the others, wincing at the noise of the crash.

He got to his feet and buttoned the only button on his coat. The middle section he held together with his hands thrust deep in his pockets and went out into the street putting his head down against the wind. He badly needed something to warm him.

His hand searched for his trouser pocket without the hole. There was a crumpled pound and what felt like a fair amount of silver. He was all right. Nobody had fleeced him the night before. Yesterday he had got his Christmas money from the Assistance and he had what would cure him today, with maybe something left for Christmas Day itself.

Strannix's bar was at the back of the Law Courts about two minutes from McGettigan's room but to McGettigan it seemed like an eternity. His thin coat flapped about his knees. He was so tall he always thought he got the worst of the wind. When he pushed open the door of the bar he felt the wave of heat and smoke and spirit smells surround him like a hug. He looked quickly behind the bar. Strannix wasn't on. It was only the barman, Hughie – a good sort. McGettigan went up to the counter and stood shivering. Hughie set him up a hot wine without a word. McGettigan put the money down on the marble slab but Hughie gestured it away.

'Happy Christmas, big lad,' he said. McGettigan nodded still unable to speak. He took the steaming glass, carrying it in both hands, to a bench at the back of the bar, and waited a moment until it cooled a bit. Then he downed it in one. He felt his insides unfurl and some of the pain begin to disappear. He got another one which he paid for.

After the second the pains had almost gone and he could unbend his long legs, look up and take in his surroundings. It was past two by the bar clock and there was a fair number in the bar. Now he saw the holly and the multi-coloured decorations and the HAPPY XMAS written white on the mirror behind the bar. There was a mixture of people at the counter, locals and ones in from the Law Courts with their waistcoats and sharp suits. They were wise-cracking and laughing and talking between each other which didn't happen every day of the year. With Strannix off he could risk going up to the bar. You never know what could happen. It was the sort of day a man could easily get drink bought for him.

He stood for a long time smiling at their jokes but nobody took any notice of him so he bought himself another hot wine and went back to his seat. It was funny how he'd forgotten that it was so near Christmas. One day was very much the same as another. Long ago Christmases had been good. There had been plenty to eat and drink. A chicken, vegetables and spuds, all at the same meal, ending up with plum-duff and custard. Afterwards the Da, if he wasn't too drunk, would serve out the mulled claret. He would heat a poker until it glowed red and sparked white when bits of dust hit it as he drew it from the fire – that was another thing, they'd always had a fire at Christmas – then he'd plunge it down the neck of the bottle and serve the wine out in cups with a spoonful of sugar in the bottom of each. Then they knew that they could go out and play with their new things until midnight if they liked, because the Ma and the Da would get full and fall asleep in their chairs. By bedtime their new things were always broken but it didn't seem to matter because you could always do something with them. Those were the days.

But there were bad times as well. He remembered the Christmas day he ended lying on the cold lino, crying in the corner, sore from head to foot after a beating Da had given him. He had knocked one of the figures from the crib on the mantlepiece and it smashed to white plaster bits on the hearth. The Da had bought the crib the day before and was a bit the worse for drink and he had laid into him with the belt – buckle and all. Even now he couldn't remember which figure it was.

McGettigan was glad he wasn't married. He could get full whenever he liked without children to worry about. He was his own master. He could have a good Christmas. He searched his pockets and took out all his money and counted it. He could afford a fair bit for Christmas Day. He knew he should get it now, just in case, and have it put to one side. Maybe he could get something to eat as well.

He went up to the counter and Hughie leaned over to hear him above the noise of the bar. When McGettigan asked him for a carry-out Hughie reminded him that it was only half-past two. Then McGettigan explained that he wanted it for Christmas. Three pint bottles of stout and three of wine.

'Will this do?' asked Hughie holding up the cheapest wine in the place and smiling. He put the bottles in a bag and left it behind the counter.

'You'll tell the boss it's for me, if he comes in,' said McGettigan.

'If Strannix comes in you'll be out on your ear,' Hughie said.

Strannix was a mean get and everybody knew it. He hated McGettigan, saying that he was the type of customer he could well do without. People like him got the place a bad name. What he really meant was that the judges and lawyers, who drank only the dearest and best – and lots of it – might object to McGettigan's sort. Strannix would strangle his grandmother for a halfpenny. it was a standing joke in the bar for the lawyers, when served with whiskey, to say, 'I'll just put a little more water in this.' Strannix was an out-and-out crook. He not only owned the bar but also the houses of half the surrounding streets. mcGettigan paid him an exorbitant amount for his room and although he hated doing it he paid as regularly as possible because he wanted to hold onto this last shred. You were beat when you didn't have a place to go. His room was the last thing he wanted to lose.

Now that he was feeling relaxed McGettigan got himself a stout and as he went back to his seat he saw Judge Boucher come in. Everybody at the bar wished him a happy Christmas in a ragged chorus. One young lawyer having wished him all the best, turned and rolled his eyes and sniggered into his hot whiskey.

Judge Boucher was a fat man, red faced with a network of tiny broken purple veins. He wore a thick, warm camel-hair overcoat and was peeling off a pair of fur-lined gloves. McGettigan hadn't realized he was bald the first time he had seen him because then he was wearing his judge's wig and sentencing him to three months for drunk and disorderly. McGettigan saw him now tilt his first gin and tonic so far back that the lemon slice hit his moustache. He slid the glass back to Hughie who refilled it. Judge Boucher cracked and rubbed his hands together and said something about how cold it was, then he pulled a piece of paper from his pocket and handed it to Hughie with a wad of money. The judge seemed to be buying for those around him so McGettigan went up close to him.

'How're ye Judge,' he said. McGettigan was a good six inches taller than the judge, but round shouldered. The judge turned and looked up at him.

'McGettigan. Keeping out of trouble, eh?' he said.

'Yis, sur. But things is bad at the minute . . . like . . . you know how it is. Now if I had the money for a bed . . .' said McGettigan fingering the stubble of his chin.

'I'll buy you no drink,' snapped the judge. 'That's the cause of your trouble, man. You look dreadful. How long is it since you've eaten?'

'It's not the food your lordship . . .' began McGettigan but he was interrupted by the judge ordering him a meat pie. He took it with mumbled thanks and went back to his seat once again.

'Happy Christmas,' shouted the judge across the bar.

Just then Strannix came in behind the bar. He was a huge muscular man and had his sleeves rolled up to his biceps. He talked in a loud Southern brogue. When he spied McGettigan he leaned over the bar hissing, 'Ya skinney big hairpin. I thought I told you if ever I caught you . . .'

'Mr Strannix,' called the judge from the other end of the counter. Strannix's face changed from venom to smile as he walked the duck-boards to where the judge stood.

'Yes Judge what can I do for you?' he said. The judge had now become professional.

'Let him be,' he said. 'Good will to all men and all that.' He laughed loudly and winked in McGettigan's direction. Strannix filled the judge's glass again and stood with a fixed smile waiting for the money.

At four o'clock the judge's car arrived for him and after much handshaking and backslapping he left. McGettigan knew his time had come. Strannix scowled over at him and with a vicious gesture of his big thumb, ordered him out.

'Hughie has a parcel for me,' said McGettigan defiantly, '. . . and it's paid for,' he added before Strannix could ask. Strannix grabbed the paper bag, then came round the counter and shoved it into McGettigan's arms and guided him firmly out the door. As the door closed McGettigan shouted, 'I hope this Christmas is your last.'

The door opened again and Strannix stuck his big face out. 'If you don't watch yourself I'll be round for the rent,' he snarled.

McGettigan spat on the pavement loud enough for Strannix to hear.

It was beginning to rain and the dark sky seemed to bring on the night more quickly. McGettigan clutched his carry-out in the crook of his arm, his exposed hand getting cold. Then he sensed something odd about the shape in the bag. There was a triangular shape in there. Not a shape he knew.

He stopped at the next street light and opened the bag. There was a bottle of whiskey, triangular in section. There was also a bottle of vodka, two bottles of gin, a bottle of brandy and what looked like some tonic.

He began to run as fast as he could. He was in bad shape, his breath rasped in his throat, his boots were filled with lead, his heart moved up and thumped in his head. As he ran he said a frantic prayer that they wouldn't catch him.

Once inside his room he set his parcel gently on the sofa, snibbed the door and lay against it panting and heaving. When he got his breath back he hunted the yard, in the last remaining daylight for some nails he knew were in a tin. Then he hammered them through the door into the jamb with wild swings of a hatchet. Then he pushed the sofa against the door and looked around the room. There was nothing else that could be moved. He sat down on the floor against the wall at the window and lined the bottles in front of him. Taking them out they tinked like full bells. In silence he waited for Strannix.

Within minutes he came, he and Judge Boucher stamping into the hallway. They battered on the door, shouting his name. Strannix shouted, 'McGettigan. We know you're in there. If you don't come out I'll kill you.

The judge's voice tried to reason, 'I bought you a meat pie, McGettigan.' He sounded genuinely hurt.

But his voice was drowned by Strannix.

'McGettigan, I know you can hear me. If you don't hand back that parcel I'll get you evicted.' There was silence. Low voices conferred outside the door. Then Strannix shouted again. 'Evicted means put out, you stupid hairpin.'

Then after some more shouting and pummelling on the door they went away, their mumbles and footsteps fading gradually.

McGettigan laughed as he hadn't laughed for years, his head thrown back against the wall. He played eeny-meeny-miney-mo with the bottles in front of him – and the whiskey won. The click of the metal seal breaking he thought much nicer than the pop of a cork. He teased himself by not drinking immediately but got up and, to celebrate, put a shilling in the meter to light the gas fire. Its white clay sections were broken and had all fallen to the bottom. The fire banged loudly because it had not been lit for such a long time, making him jump back and laugh. Then McGettigan pulled the sofa up to the fire and kicked off his boots. His toes showed white through the holes in his socks and the steam began to rise from his feet. A rectangle of light fell on the floor from the street-lamp outside the uncurtained window. The whiskey was red and gold in the light from the gas fire.

He put the bottle to his head and drank. The heat from inside him met the warmth of his feet and they joined in comfort. Again and again he put the bottle to his head and each time he lowered it he listened to the music of the back-slop. Soon the window became a bright diamond and he wondered if it was silver rain drifting in the halo of the lamp or if it was snow for Christmas. Choirs of boy sopranos sang carols and McGettigan, humming, conducted slowly with his free hand and the room bloomed in the darkness of December.

CURTAINS FOR CHRISTMAS

BRIAN LYNCH

E dward smiled across the Musak enchanted room at Michael the porter. Michael, short, fat and hurrying, waggled his fingers at the ceiling as if incredulous of how busy they were, and went back to the reception desk.

'That's some bleedin' goer,' he said to the bell-boy.

'Who is?'

'That Norman fella hasn't stopped at the gargle since he came.'

'What fella?'

'Edward. Mr. Norman.'

'That fella. What about him?'

The bell-boy was the oldest man in the hotel. He was so old he remembered the Black and Tans, drunk all night, firing guns into the ceiling or at the chandeliers. There wasn't any carry-on like that nowadays.

They slumped together on the desk before the battling door which opened and closed windily on the parcel-laden crowds thronging through to the lounge and the bar. It was Christmas Eve. Most of the people seemed to be sleep-walking, distracted, concentrating, yearning like animals for somewhere to sit and something to drink. Michael and the bell-boy watched them as if at some vast controlled experiment.

Edward was sitting in the lounge, alone, back to the unlit fire. He was watching and smiling. He knotted his square strong hands behind his close-cropped

144

head and tilted on his chair. The light caught the bright gold of the sovereign signet-ring on his loittle finger and his tight blue sweater rode up, generously displaying the greyness of his belly hard enough with muscle, loose enough with all the pints of Smithwick's ale he'd been drinking, for – was it days or weeks or months?

The man sitting nearest looked at the belly and then at the face and then looked away again. His wife didn't notice, dazedly quick-sipping her hot whiskey like a flustered hen. Her fur hat with the flaps tied under the chin was crooked, thick feathers of hair escaping on all sides. Edward smiled. He knew and he listened. There was a sound in his head like the roaring of the sea on a distant beach.

The lounge of Flynn's Hotel was painted yellow. The carpet was brown, green and yellow. The curtains were red, the lightshades orange. Some of the older chairs were upholstered in green leather. The banquettes lining the walls were new, black plastic leather.

The waitresses, still dressed as if of old, in black with little white aprons, brought drinks, tea and coffee and sandwiches on silver trays. Some of the pots, jugs and bowls were battered silver. Some were stainless steel, narrowing towards the tops, the handles inset with dark simulated wood, Swedish by design. The high ceiling was hung with paper chains and bits of tinsel.

'Not a parish priest in sight' Mr. Grealy said to his married daughter as she joined him from her shopping. 'Place used to be thick with them. I remember you couldn't spit here once for fear of committing sacrilege!'

'How many pints of stout have you had?'

'This is my first glass.'

'Could I have a coffee please' she said to Mr. Lawrence, the lounge manager.

'Certainly, madam. One coffee is it?'

They understood each other instantly. She paused and looked briefly to the left and right of her. There was only one of her.

'One coffee. With cream.'

He bowed. She put out a restraining hand, almost touching his arm but not quite.

'And a very small glass of water. I think I'm getting a cold.' She said this to her father. 'And I want to take one of these tablets.'

'Certainly madam.'

He bowed again, sympathetically, and went away to return swiftly with coffee and a half-pint glass of water. 'This is not what I asked for!'

'One coffee and a glass of water madam.'

'I asked for a small glass of water.'

'This is the smallest glass we have.'

'Do you call that a small glass?'

'Shall I change it for you, madam?'

'However,' she said, 'it'll do.'

She poured off water into her father's almost empty glass of stout.

'Now.' she said, 'If you could take that away and bring me another glass of stout. No, wait. And a ham sandwich, I think we'll do for the moment.'

Mr. Lawrence brushed back the wings of his silvery hair with both hands, removed some empty cups and used plates, left the water and stout mixing sickeningly together, and resolved, smiling tightly, never to return.

Edward finished his ninth pint of Smithwick's, stretched, picked up the glass and went through to the bar for another. The three barmaids entwined at the cash-register like Graces disentangled themselves.

Even standing up, Edward's sweater was too small and exposed a couple of inches of flesh, a belt above the thick belt of his jeans.

'Give us a smile, ducks,' he said. Edward was happy. Not to be happy was, he felt, a moral fault, but the fact that his experience in showing happiness had not guaranteed reciprocity in others added an edge to his good nature that his smiling only accentuated.

Edward felt someone behind him trying to get in at the bar. He flicked the pressure away with his hip. A small man, Brendan Hartigan, staggered slightly against the man next to him. Two of the barmaids saw the move.

'Could I have,' Brendan said, 'a hot whickey please and a cup of coffee please.'

'No coffee in the bar. You'll have to go into the lounge for that.'

The girl who spoke had not taken her eyes off Edward flexing and cracking his muscle-bound fingers.

'Holy Jesus,' Brendan said under his breath and went back to Paula, surrounded by packages, heavily pregnant, sunk deep in the soft tweed of an under-sprung armchair.

'We'll have to go into the god-damned lounge if you want coffee.'

He rewound the eight feet of his thick bright scarf around his neck in annoyance, as if going on a long cold journey. They threaded their way along the narrow bar, stood in the crowded lounge, spotted a couple leaving and squeezed past Mr. Grealy to a vacant spot on the black plastic. The girl who was serving a ham sandwich and a glass of stout took their order.

All this time Mrs. Winnie Ormsby had been descending the stairs. Now she stood in the door of

147

the lounge. Mouth clamped shut, breathing hard through her nose, one hand pressed to her side, the other held a little in front of her. She started off again, thin legs wavering. Her turquoise skirt hung lopsidedly because the zip had caught in a clump of pink slip. Her bright red cardigan was wrongly buttoned. It was all due to her eyes. A thick, loose wad of cottonwool, stuck to forehead and cheek with plaster, pressed against one lens of her spectacles, lifting the arm so that it didn't rest on her ear.

When she came in sight of the bar she held up the key of her room for identification until they gave her her large Scotch. Then she headed for her corner. An arm encircled her shoulders and turned her around.

'I have a party for there this minute.' said Mr. Laurence.

He put her gently on a stool in the middle of the room beside a tiny table.

'This is a mad country,' Mr. Grealy's daughter said, turning back her gaze.

'Where do they get the money, that's what I want to know. Daddy, don't eat my crusts, you know I don't like it. Where do they get it? I've never seen a country where they could drink more than Ireland.'

'I couldn't say so.'

She dropped the second of her big Rubex tablets into the water and watched it fizz angrily.

'Is it any wonder we're in the state we're in? Nothing but bars and bars and more bars.'

'I hear the asylums are full of publicans.'

'And not from poverty. Not from poverty. Some of the people wouldn't think twice about going out and spending ten pounds in one night on drink.'

'And more maybe.'

'And more. And not one of them would dream of spending ten pounds on dinner in a restaurant. That's

148

what has the country the way it is. The people wouldn't dream of eating.'

Edward stood up, stretched again and went to the lavatory, smiling. Mr. Lawrence, going about with his eyes lowered to avoid further orders, first felt a vick-like arm groping his shoulder and then looked up into a pair of gleaming red eyes.

'You're run off your feet, ducks,' Edward said.

'Thank you, Mr. Norman,' said Mr. Lawrence.

'Have one on me, have a brandy.'

'Thank you, sir, very pleased to, much obliged.'

A pound note was pressed into the breast pocket of his shiny evening jacket.

'Compliments of the season, sir.'

'Enough said.'

'Rotten crowd of bleeders, what?'

Mr. Lawsrence saw the face press closer and felt the hot breath on his nose. He lowered his eyes.

'Don't be like a blue-arsed fly then.' There was a ghastly pause.

'What you say, cock? Bleeding Irish, that's all they are. Here.'

Mr. Lawrence saw another pound note crush down on the first one.

'Have a brandy or something. On me.'

Edward took his arm away, cannoned into an ivory-faced man and burst out through the door.

Mrs. Winnie Ormsby held her key over her head, turned towards the girls behind the bar, found it was her wrong eye and turned again. Mr. Lawrence, raging with relief came up behind and snatched the key from her hand which remained stiffly in the air.

'Now, then, Mrs. Ormsby, what's this, what's this?'

'Here I am love. Not there sweet-heart, here.'

'You can put your hand down now, you silly old dear.'

Slowly she turned and wordlessly raised the glass that was clutched in her clubbed arthritic fingers.

'One of our oldest residents,' Mr. Lawrence said. 'Faithful and true, right up to the end.'

'Couldn't I have another coffee and a hot whiskey, please,' Brendan said.

'And I'll have another coffee, Daddy, do you think you'll manage another glass of Guinness?'

'Yes, well, another glass of Guinness.'

Mr. Grealy's daughter thrust the almost empty glass into Mr. Lawrence's hand.

'There's no rush, madam,' Mr. Lawrence said easily, smiling politely and putting the glass back on the table. The girl he called over took the order again.

Mr. Lawrence hovered and then descended. There was, after all, one thing he should do straight away.

'Excuse me, sir,' he said to Mr. Grealy, 'if you could just stand up for a moment.'

Obediently Mr. Grealy stood up. Kneeling on the banquette, Mr. Lawrence pulled the cord which drew the red mock-velvet curtains. Then brushing his hands together he withdrew.

Edward, coming back from the lavatory, bumped into him and said, 'Do you come here often, darling, or is it the mating season?' and went off, laughing, to order the next pint.

Paula shivered first. She pulled up the collar of her coat and sank down further on her heavy body. 'There's a draught,' she said.

'I feel it too,' Brendan said.

The lounge was more crowded now and warm, but they felt a cold thin shaft of air down their necks.

'Do you feel it too?' Mr. Grealy's daughter asked.

Brendan twisted around and drew the curtain aside.

'It's the fan,' he said. 'See, the fan in the window.

It's all right when the curtains are open, but now he's drawn them the draught comes down and gets under the edge.'

Mrs. Ormsby spoke: 'My eye hurts,' she said. She meant her good eye.

'Call that man,' Mr. Grealy's daughter instructed. Brendan called out, raising his hand like the timid schoolboy he once was. Mr. Lawrence passed by. Eventually a girl came, but she said she'd have to speak to the manager.

'Please ask him to come in, like a good girl,' Mr. Grealy's daughter said. Mr. Lawrence came eagerly.

'Now, then, sir, it's not that bad, is it? A little draught, you say.'

'My wife is cold.'

'I'm very sorry sir, we have to think of the other customers.'

Brendan was lost and didn't know what to say. This was the sort of thing he hated. He felt that his head had grown huge and that everyone was looking at it.

'It's hurting that old woman's eye,' he said at last.

'Sure it has cotton wool over it,' Mr. Lawrence said, chuckling.

'Walked into an open door, didn't we, Mrs. Ormsby? Naughty thing. I'm sorry sir, perhaps you can find another seat.'

He disappeared. Brendan sank back. Mr. Grealy turned the bottom of his glass thorugh wet circles. The draught brought a tear to Mrs. Ormsby's good eye. It rembled on the glaciated lip of her cheekbone. Mr. Grealy's daughter's eye did not water. It gleamed. She beckoned over the girl.

'What's your name pet?' she asked. The girl involuntarily brought her hands together in front of her and her bowels turned over.

'Jacinta, miss, Jacinta Higgins, miss.'

151

'What's the manager's name, Jacinta?'

'Mr. Lawrence, miss.'

'Good. Now Jacinta, run over to Mr. Lawrence like a good girl and tell him I want to see him. This instant.'

'Can we go home now? Mr. Grealy asked, but it was already too late.

'Can I help you madam?' inquired Mr. Lawrence.

'Pull back the curtains please.'

'Excuse me madam?'

'There is a draught here. Kindly draw the curtains.'

'The curtains? These curtains?' Mr. Lawrence raised his shoulders and held both of his palms upwards like a priest before a congregation. 'I'm sorry, madam, very sorry, but it's dark now, you see, I must draw the curtains when it's dark.'

'There is a draught here,' Mr. Grealy's daughter said. 'Don't you feel it?'

'I'm sorry, madam.'

'A wind, a breeze. Do you know what that is?'

'You don't have to explain it to me, madam, with respect. But I think you're exaggerating a little fresh air.'

'There is a gale coming through that window.'

'Look,' said Brendan, 'the curtains are lifting with it.' The curtains swayed slightly. The smile faded from Mr. Lawrence's face.

'You're a man, aren't you, you're not hurt by a little fresh air, are you?'

'We would like the curtains drawn,' Mr. Grealy's daughter said in an amused voice. Mrs. Ormsby bent her head into her glass as if it were an asthmatic's mask.

'I'm terribly sorry, madam,' Mr. Lawrence said, 'I would like to be of assistance, but I have my orders.'

'Orders, what orders?'

She slammed her glass down on the formica-topped

table and the remains of her Rubex shot up into the air and dived back down again as soon as they could. A ghastly silence ensued. It was as if sound had been suddenly removed from the world. Mr. Grealy's daughter spoke, conversationally: 'I said draw the curtains.' Then her voice swelled up again: 'Now draw them.'

'No need to raise your voice,' Mr. Lawrence stood his ground. 'Orders are orders, after all, where would we be without them?'

'Look here,' Brendan cried. The blood rushing to his head seemed to drive him to his feet. He scrambled down the banquette. His elbow hit Mr. Grealy on the temple and sent his glasses flying. Clawing at the curtains he tried to find the proper cords, but when he pulled nothing happened.

'Brendan,' he heard Paula scream. The next thing he knew his feet were flailing the air and his chest was being crushed by a mighty arm.

'Don't hit an old man,' Edward Norman's voice, warm and fermenting said mildly in his ear. Brendan, in terror, feeling his rib-cage crack, gasping for breath, kicked out frantically. One heel caught Mr. Grealy flush on his blue-red nose, bringing forth a gush of blood. The other heel caught Mr. Grealy's daughter cleanly on the chin. Her arms went out wide and her chair went over backwards.

Paula's face came near and Edward pushed it away, he thought gently. Brendan attempted to turn. His elbow hit Edward's jaw. Edward felt a gold filling break off. Enraged, he whirled Brendan around and flung him from him across the room. Brendan's clutching hand held on to the curtain cord as if it were a last lifeline, as he flew through the air. He landed on a table full of glasses. The curtain rail, aluminium, with a terrible sound was torn off the wall and speared

Mrs. Ormsby directly in the middle of her forehead.

There was silence. No one said or did anything for a moment. Then, with a sigh, a large star-shaped piece of plaster fell from the ceiling on Edward Norman's cropped head.

Unharmed, Mr. Lawrence stood knee-deep in the human wreckage, trying desperately to persuade himself that the rictus of pleasure on his face was the purest anguish. Desperately he rubbed his hands together as if he were trying to mould in the hairy cushioned pads of his palms and appropriate expression for his features.

'Orders, orders,' he said over and over with a frantic giggle. 'I have my orders.'

Edward stood stock still, head and shoulders sprinkled with plaster dust like theatrical snow, eyes fixed with dog-numb adoration on what he recognised at last what was his master's voice. His master's voice, freed from the awful sanity of restraint, now rose to a piercing goatish bellow of the purest, most panic-stricken merriment.

Everyone who was capable of movement moved, either towards the door, where a screaming cork of bodies clawed and clogged, or against any wall into which a back might transubstantiate. Even in this hubbub Edward began to hear another sound. At first it was like a low humming and he couldn't work out what was causing it, but as it increased to a loud drum solo and then to a terrible pounding which made the floor vibrate violently, his eyes were drawn from Mr. Lawrence's howling mouth to his feet. Tiny feet they were and utterly immobile – except that is, for the heels which were beating up and down in a blurred joyous tattoo. In a moment they reached such a speed that, like the wheels of buckboard wagons in cowboy films, they seemed not to move at all and then to go backward to their motion. Most wonderful of all, this allowed Edward to see the heels of Mr. Lawrence's boots were – what else? – Cuban.

Unheard, unseen, somewhere else, Paula began to moan. Something far more interesting was happening to her.

CHRISTMAS

JOHN McGAHERN

As well as a railway ticket they gave me a letter before I left the Home to work for Moran. They warned me to give the letter unopened to Moran, which was why I opened it on the train; it informed Moran that since I was a ward of state if I caused trouble or ran away he was to contact the police at once. I tore it up, since it occurred to me that I might as well cause trouble or run away, resolving to say I lost it if asked, but Moran did not ask for any letter.

Moran and his wife treated me well. The food was more solid than at the Home, a roast always on Sundays, and when the weather grew hard they took me to the town and bought me Wellingtons and an overcoat and a cap with flaps that came down over the ears. After the day's work when Moran had gone to the pub, I was free to sit at the fire, while Mrs. Moran knitted, and listened to the wireless – what I enjoyed most were the plays – and Mrs. Moran had told me she was knitting me a pullover for Christmas. Sometimes she asked me about life at the Home and I'd tell her and she'd sigh, 'You must be very glad to be with us instead,' and I would tell her, which was true, that I was. I mostly went to bed before Moran came from the pub as they often quarrelled then, and I considered I had no place in that part of their lives.

Moran made his living by buying cheap branches, or uncommercial timber the sawmills couldn't use, and cutting them up to sell as firewood. I delivered the timber with an old jennet Moran had bought from the tinkers; the jennet squealed, a very human squeal, any time a fire of branches was lit and ran, about the only time he did run, to stand in rigid contentment with his nostrils in the thick of the wood smoke. When Moran was in good humour it amused him greatly to light a fire specially to see the jennet's excitement at the prospect of smoke.

There was no reason this life shouldn't have gone on for long but for a stupid wish on my part, which set off an even more stupid wish in Mrs. Grey, and what happened has struck me ever since as usual when people look to each other for their happiness or whatever it is called. Mrs. Grey was Moran's best customer. She'd come from America and built the huge house on top of Mounteagle after her son had been killed in aerial combat over Italy.

The thaw overhead in the bare branches had stopped, the evening we filled that load for Mrs. Grey; there was no longer the dripping on the dead leaves, the wood clamped in the silence of white frost except for the racket some bird made in the undergrowth. Moran carefully built the last logs above the crates of the cart and I threw him in the bag of hay that made the load look bigger than it was. 'Don't forget to call at Murphy's for her paraffin,' he said. 'No, I'll not forget.' 'She's bound to tip you well this Christmas. We could use money for the Christmas.' He'd use it to pour drink down his gullet. 'Must be time to be moving,' I said. 'It'll be night before you're there,' he answered.

The cart rocked over the roots between the trees, cold steel of the bridle ring in the hand close to the rough black lips, steam of the breath wasting on the air to either side. We went across the paddocks to the path round the lake, the wheels cutting two tracks on the white stiff grass, crush of the grass yielding to the iron. I had to open the wooden gate to the pass. The small shod hooves wavered between the two ridges of green inside the wheeltracks on the pass as the old body swayed to each drive of the shafts, as the wheels fell from rut to rut.

The lake was frozen over, a mirror fouled by white blotches of the springs, and rose streaks from the sun impaled on the firs of Oakport across the bay.

The chainsaw started up in the wood again, he'd saw while there was light. 'No joke to make a living, a drink or two for some relief, all this ballsing. May be better if we stayed in bed, conserve our energy, eat less,' but in spite of all he said he went on buying the branches cheap from McAnnish after the boats had taken the trunks down the river to the mill.

I tied the jennet to the chapel gate and crossed to Murphy's shop.

'I want Mrs. Grey's paraffin.'

The shop was full of men, they sat on the counter or on wooden fruit boxes and upturned buckets along the walls. They used to trouble me at first: I supposed it little different from going into a shop in a strange country without its language, but they learned they couldn't take a rise out of me, that was their phrase. They used to lob tomatoes at the back of my head in the hope of some reaction, but they left me mostly alone when they saw none was forthcoming. If I felt anything for them it was a contempt tempered by fear: and I was here, and they were there.

'You want her paraffin, do you? I know the paraffin I'd give her if I got your chance,' Joe Murphy said from the centre of the counter where he presided, and a loyal guffaw rose from around the walls.

'Her proper paraffin,' someone shouted, and it drew even more applause, and when it died a voice asked, 'Before you get off the counter, Joe, throw us an orange?' They bought chocolate and fruit as token payment for their stay. Joe stretched to the shelf and threw the orange to the man who sat on a bag of Spanish onions. As he stretched forward to catch the fruit the red string bag collapsed and he came heavily down on the onions. 'You want to bruise those onions with your dirty awkward arse. Will you pay for them now, will you?' Joe shouted as he swung his thick legs down from the counter. 'Everybody's out for their onions these days,' the man tried to defend himself with a nervous laugh as he fixed the string bag upright and changed his seat to an orange box.

'You've had your onions: now pay for them.'

'Make him pay for his onions,' they shouted.

'You must give her her paraffin first.' Joe took the tin and went to the barrel raised on flat blocks in the corner, and turned the copper tap.

'Now give her the proper paraffin. It's Christmas time,' Joe said again as he screwed the cap tight on the tin, the limp black hair falling across the bloated face.

'Her proper paraffin,' the approving cheer followed me out the door.

'He never moved a muscle, the little fucker. Those Homeboys are a bad piece of work,' I heard with much satisfaction as I stowed the tin of paraffin securely among the logs of the cart. Ice, over the potholes of the road, was catching the first stars. Lights of bicycles, it was a confession night, hesitantly approached out of the night. Though exposed isn the full glare of their lamps I was unable to recognise the bicyclists as they pedalled past in dark shapes behind their lamps and this made raw the fear I'd felt but had held down in the shop. I took a stick and beat the reluctant jennet into pulling the load uphill as fast as he was able.

After I'd stacked the logs in the fuel shed I went and knocked on the back door to see where they wanted

159

me to put the paraffin. Mrs. Grey opened the door.

'It's the last load until Christmas,' I said as I put the tin down.

'I haven't forgotten.' She smiled and held out a pound note.

'I'd rather not take it.' It was there the first mistake was made, playing for higher stakes.

'You must have something, besides the firewood you've brought us so many messages from the village that we don't know what we'd have done without you.'

'I don't want money.'

'Then what would you like me to give you for Christmas?'

'Whatever you'd prefer to give me.' I thought *prefer* was well put for a Homeboy.

'I'll have to give it some thought then,' she said as I led the jennet out of the yard delirious with stupid happiness.

'You got the paraffin and logs there without trouble?' Moran beamed when I came in to the smell of hot food. He'd changed into good clothes and was finishing his meal at the head of the big table in tired contentment.

'There was no trouble,' I answered.

'You've fed and put in the jennet?'

'I gave him crushed oats.'

'I bet you Mrs. Grey was pleased.'

'She seemed pleased.'

He'd practically his hand out. 'You got something good out of it then?'

'No.'

'You mean to say she gave you nothing?'

'Not tonight but maybe she will before Christmas.'

'Maybe she will but she always gave a pound with the last load before,' he said suspiciously. His early

160

contentment was gone.

He took his cap and coat to go for a drink or two for some relief.

'If there's an international crisis in the next few hours you know where I'll be found,' he said to Mrs. Moran as he left.

Mrs. Grey came Christmas Eve with a large box. She smelled of scent and gin and wore a fur coat. She refused a chair saying she'd to rush, and asked me to untie the red twine and paper.

A toy airplane stood inside the box. It was painted white and blue and the tyres smelled of new rubber.

'Why don't you wind it up and see it go?'

I looked at the idiotically smiling face, the tear-brimmed eyes.

'Wind it up for Mrs. Grey,' I heard Mrs. Moran's voice.

While the horrible hurt of the toy was changing to rage I was able to do nothing. Moran took the toy from my hand and wound it up. A light flashed on and off on the tail as it raced across the cement and the propellors turned.

'It was too much for you to bring,' Moran said in his polite voice.

'I thought it was rather nice when he refused the money. My own poor boy loved nothing better than model airplanes for Christmas,' she was again on the verge of tears.

'We all still feel for that tragedy,' Moran said and insisted, 'Thank Mrs. Grey for such a lovely present. It's far too good.'

'I think it's useless,' I could no longer hold back rage, and began to sob. I have only a vague memory afterwords except the voice of Moran accompanying her to the door with excuses and apologies.

'I should have known better than to trust a

Homeboy,' Moran said when he came back. 'Not only did you do me out of the pound but you go and insult the woman and her dead son. You're going to make quick time back to where you came from, my tulip.'

Moran stirred the airplane with his boot as if he wished to kick it but dared not out of respect for the money it had cost.

'Well you'll have a good flight in it this Christmas.'

The two-hour bell went for Midnight Mass, and as Moran hurried for the pub to get drinks before Mass, Mrs. Moran started to strip the windows of curtains and to set a single candle to burn in each window. Later, as we made our way to the church, candles burned in the windows of all the houses and the church was ablaze with light. I was ashamed of the small old woman, after they'd identify me with her, as we walked up between the crowded benches to where a steward directed us to a seat in the women's side-altar. In the smell of burning wax and flowers and damp stone, I got out the brown beads and the black prayerbook with the gold cross on the cover they'd given me in the Home and began to prepare for the hours of boredom Midnight Mass meant; but it did not turn out that way, it was to be a lucky Christmas. A drunken policeman, Guard Mullins, had slipped past the stewards on guard at the door and into the women's sidechapel. As Mass began he started to tell the school-teacher's wife how available her arse had been for handling while she'd worked in the bar before assuming the fur coat of respectability, 'And now, O lordy me a prize rose garden wouldn't get a luk in edgeways with its grandeur.' The stewards had a hurried consultation whether to eject him or not and decided it'd probably cause less scandal to leave him as he was. They seemed right for he quietened into a drunken stupor until the Monsignor climbed into the

162

pulpit to begin his annual hour of the season of peace and glad tidings. As soon as he began, 'In the name of the Father and of the Son and of the Holy Ghost. This Christmas, my dearly beloved children in Christ, I wish . . .' Mullins woke to applaud with a hearty, 'Hear, hear. I couldn't approve more. You're a man after my own heart. Down with the hypocrites!' The Monsignor looked towards the policeman and then at the stewards, but as he was greeted by another, 'Hear, hear!' he closed his notes and in a voice of acid wished everybody a holy and happy Christmas, and angrily climbed from the pulpit to conclude the shortest Midnight Mass the church had ever known. It was not, though, the end of the entertainment. As the communicants came from the rails Mullins singled out the tax collector, who walked down the aisle with eyes closed, bowed head, and hands rigidly joined, to shout, 'There's the biggest hypocrite in the parish,' which delighted almost everybody.

I thought of Mullins as my friend as I went past the lighted candles in the window, and felt for the first time proud to be a ward of state. I avoided Moran and his wife and from the attic I listened with glee to them criticizing Mullins. When the voices died I came quietly down to take a box of matches and the airplane and go to the jennet's stable. I gathered dry straw in a heap and as I lit it and the smoke rose he gave his human squeal until I untied him and he was able to put his nostrils in the thick smoke. By the light of the burning straw I put the blue and white goy against the wall and started to kick. Each kick I gave, it seemed a new sweetness was injected into my blood. For such a pretty toy it took few kicks to reduce it to shapelessness, and then in the last flames of the straw I jumped on it on the stable floor where the jennet was already nosing me to put more straw on the dying fire.

I was glad, as I quietened, that I'd torn up in the train the letter that I was supposed to give unopened to Moran. I felt a new life for me had already started to grow out of the ashes, out of the stupidity of human wishes.